FAMILY, FRIENDS
and
FATALITIES

EMERALD FINN

FINESSE SOLUTIONS

Cover design by Wicked Good Book Designs
Published by Finesse Solutions Pty Ltd
2025/01
ISBN: 9781925607147

Author's note: This book was written and produced in Australia and uses
British/Australian spelling conventions, such as "colour" instead of
"color", and "-ise" endings instead of "-ize" on words like "realise".

A catalogue record for this book is available from the National Library of
Australia

For the readers who waited so patiently for another Charlie adventure

CHAPTER 1

PRIYA TOSSED BACK HER CHARDONNAY AND SET THE EMPTY GLASS down with brittle precision, her dark eyes defiant. For a reporter who spent so much time nosing into other people's business, she sure didn't like having the tables turned on her. But this wasn't *The Sunny Bay Star*, and she didn't have the upper hand here. "We should talk about something else."

We were in the bar of the grand old Metropole Hotel, gathered around a table that would have given us a glorious view of Sunrise Bay if there was any daylight to see by. But it was almost nine o'clock on a Friday night, and outside the tall windows along one wall, the ocean had disappeared into the dark, leaving only the ceaseless shushing of its waves to remind us of its presence. The room was only half full tonight, the usual mix of locals and hotel guests seated at the tables or chatting by the long wooden bar. The relaxed hum of Friday night conversations swirled around us in the warm glow of the art deco lamps.

Aunt Evie leaned forward in her chair while I settled back, anticipating fireworks, and took another sip of my cocktail.

"Nonsense," Aunt Evie said firmly. Aunt Evie said most things firmly. She was a tiny woman with a big personality and an opinion on everything. Her opinions on Priya's current disagreement with her mother were no secret to any of us around the table. "It's high time you mended this breach with Amina."

The large gold hoops dangling from Priya's ears flashed in the light as she tossed her head. "It's her own fault for trying to set me up with every rando she thinks would make a suitable husband. I don't care."

"Priya Nayar," Aunt Evie scolded. "That's not true. Of course you care. She's your mother."

"We need popcorn for this," Heidi murmured, leaning closer to me with a conspiratorial grin.

Usually, it was just Priya and I meeting for drinks. We were about the same age, and had become such good friends that I often forgot I'd only met her last year, when I first moved to Sunrise Bay. Back then, my beloved Aunt Evie was the only person in town I knew, but she'd quickly changed that, introducing me to her circle of friends and helping me settle into my new home.

Tonight, Priya had talked Heidi, Aunt Evie, and Andrea into joining us, despite Aunt Evie's protests that she was too old, Heidi's that she had to get up early for work in the morning, and Andrea's that she'd really rather be at home curled up with a book.

Andrea was the town librarian, so that might have been true, if a little unflattering to us as her friends. It was also true that Heidi had to get up early—but then, as the mother of energetic six-year-old twins, she always did, so it wasn't much of an excuse.

And as for Aunt Evie saying she was too old, well, Priya had simply laughed in her face and told her to pull the other one, it played "Jingle Bells". Aunt Evie was a force of nature who only played the little old lady card when it suited her.

Priya certainly wasn't laughing now. Once the talk had come around to the ongoing chill in her relationship with her mum, her mouth had set in a stubborn line with which I'd become all too familiar. Last December, she'd concocted a scheme to stop her mother's constant match-making by passing my neighbour Jack off as her boyfriend. Everyone but Priya had been able to see that it wouldn't end well, but we hadn't been able to talk her out of it.

Just as we now couldn't persuade her to apologise to her mother and try to mend fences.

"I must admit," Heidi said, flicking a long blond plait over her shoulder, "I never expected Amina to hold a grudge this long."

Amina had discovered the deception just before Christmas, and it was now July. That was seven months of tension in what had been a close-knit family.

"Ha!" Priya fiddled with a spare coaster, tapping it impatiently against the dark wood of the table. "If holding grudges were an Olympic sport, my mother would take the gold medal. She'll hold that against me until the day she dies."

"Nonsense," Aunt Evie said again. "Amina loves you. A proper apology and a good, long chat to clear the air would work wonders." Her long blue earrings danced as she nodded emphatically.

"I *have* apologised! Several times, in fact. But if you think that makes a difference, you don't know my mother. She's as stubborn as they come."

"Pot, meet kettle," Andrea murmured, a smile tugging at the corner of her mouth. She'd come straight from the library when it closed at eight, and had her dark hair up in the casual bun she usually wore to work. Normally, she had Friday afternoons off; she only agreed to join us for drinks because she'd been filling in for a sick coworker. Otherwise, she would have been curled up with that book hours ago.

"I'm not stubborn," Priya said, wide-eyed with outrage at the very suggestion.

The rest of us burst out laughing.

"I'm not!" she insisted, which only made us laugh harder.

"Oh, I needed a good laugh," Aunt Evie said eventually, wiping tears from her eyes.

Priya was glaring at us all, so Heidi stepped in to smooth the waters, as she so often did. "Let's call it *determined*, then," she said, with the practised diplomacy that years of twin-wrangling had given her. "But, you know, sometimes it's better to be happy than to be right."

I nodded, impressed. People often underestimated Heidi. She wasn't tall, and often wore her blond hair in childlike plaits. Together with her enthusiastic outlook on life and her boundless energy, she could come across as someone much younger and even a bit naïve. But in fact, she was a shrewd businesswoman whose shop, Toy Stories, was one of the busiest in town, and she ran her household with the same ruthless efficiency.

"I'm not unhappy," Priya said. "I just think she should admit it when she's wrong. Anyway, enough about me. How was everyone else's week?"

I didn't believe her. Sure, she wasn't sobbing herself to sleep every night, but Priya was used to a close, if sometimes exasperated, relationship with her mother. Their current coldness had to be hurting.

Andrea launched into one of her funny stories about the antics of the library patrons, but I got distracted partway through by a tall, fair-haired man in a shirt bearing a lurid, flamingo-covered design. He was at the bar having a quiet but intense conversation with a woman I recognised.

I'd met her briefly that very afternoon, when I'd come to the hotel to do a quick photo shoot for a company that was running their conference here. She was the personal assistant of the CEO, and she'd organised a roomful of people for a group photo with an ease that suggested she was very good at her job. Her name was Krystal Dendekker —*Krystal with a K, not a C, sweetie*, she'd said—and she had a sleek, well-groomed beauty that reminded me of a cat. Perfectly manicured nails, perfectly made-up face. Blond, waist-length hair that fell in elegant waves, as though she'd just stepped out of the salon. Since this afternoon, she'd changed out of her business attire into a red dress that clung to her curves and a matching pair of sky-high stilettos.

She didn't look at all happy, though. Neither did the man, for that matter. I hadn't seen him at the conference, but they evidently knew each other well, considering how closely he was leaning in to speak to her.

"Charlie?" Heidi nudged me, and I realised I must have checked out of the conversation because everyone was looking at me expectantly. "Have you read the book?"

"The book?"

"*Madame Bovary*," Andrea said. "For book club. You *are* coming on Tuesday, aren't you?"

"Of course."

I must have looked guilty because Andrea gave me a stern look. "You haven't read it yet, have you?"

"I definitely have. At least, I've started it. I must have read a good fifty pages."

Andrea raised a particularly judgy eyebrow.

"Maybe sixty?" I ventured.

Heidi laughed. "Sixty pages! You've barely got past the introductions."

"It just seems ... a little bleak?"

Our book club only had one rule for choosing the books we read: the author had to be dead. So far that meant we'd read a lot of stuff that had been written in the 1800s. If the books were any indication, most people in those times lived in a permanent funk of depression. It made reading a bit of a downer, however worthy Andrea said the books were, or however masterful the prose.

"Ha!" Priya snorted. "Wait till you get to the end. You haven't seen bleak until you've seen a woman kill herself over a bunch of worthless men who don't live up to the guys she reads about in romance novels."

"Priya!" Heidi flapped her hands. "*Spoilers!*"

Priya shrugged. "What? She's not going to read it."

At the bar, Krystal got up to leave, but her companion grabbed her arm to stop her. There was something in the way he did it that raised my hackles.

"Ladies," Andrea cut in. "Let's leave our discussion of the novel until we get to book club, hmmm?"

I laughed, forcing my attention back to my friends and away from whatever was going on at the bar. Other people's relationships were none of my business. "Spoil away! There's a reason I prefer fantasy novels—at least I mostly get a happy ending. Why are all the classics so gloomy?"

"Jane Austen wasn't gloomy," Aunt Evie pointed out.

"True." I'd enjoyed *Pride and Prejudice*, which had been my introduction to the book club, but since then, the pickings had been slim indeed. "Whatever happened to reading *Frankenstein*? That was supposed to be on the schedule, but somehow another Dickens novel snuck in instead." Granted, *Frankenstein* would probably turn out to be just as gloomy as *Madame Bovary*, but at least it was in my wheelhouse, being science fiction.

A sudden hubbub of raised voices drew more eyes than mine to the little tableau at the bar. Krystal snatched her arm from the man's grip in a violent movement and stormed out. Her companion ran a frustrated hand through his hair. When he noticed we were watching, he downed the rest of his beer and followed her through the open doors into the foyer.

"Who was that?" Aunt Evie asked, her gossip radar all a-quiver. "Does anyone know?"

The others shrugged.

"I met the woman earlier," I said. "She works for a company called Klein's World of Kristmas. It's a small, family-owned company."

"That makes ... Christmas decorations?" Aunt Evie asked.

"Big ones for shopping centres," I said. "They handle all the design and installation. They're having some kind of conference here this weekend, and they asked me to come in today to take some photos. The old guy who owns it recognised me from that article you wrote about me, Priya."

"'Local Photographer Exposes Thief in a Flash'?" Her eyes gleamed. "Some of my best work."

"Yes. *You're the one who found that necklace, aren't you?* he said. Seemed to think it was a grand joke how the thief managed to make off with it in a ballroom full of witnesses. You would have thought I was a celebrity, he was so pleased to meet me. I honestly think that's why they hired me for the photo shoot today. He wanted me to tell him all about it."

Priya shrugged. "As long as he pays the bills."

"Well, you are *kind* of a celebrity," Heidi said loyally. "At least around Sunny Bay."

Aunt Evie nodded. "Better than that awful Kelly woman."

I sighed. Kelly Parmenter was a model—tall, tanned, with long blond hair and cheekbones you could cut yourself on. A slightly more upmarket version of the woman who'd just stormed out of the bar, actually, at least as far as looks went. She was no superstar, but she was the closest thing to a celebrity that tiny Sunrise Bay could boast, and the locals were always interested in stories of her overseas triumphs. She partied hard, living the high life in glamorous locations, and I'd never expected to have anything to do with her.

Unfortunately for me, she was also the ex-wife of my current partner. It was still a mystery to me how a genuinely decent guy like Curtis could ever have ended up with a snake like Kelly, but that's hormones for you, I guess. In his defence, he'd been a lot younger when they got married, and the marriage hadn't lasted that long.

Long enough to produce one of my favourite people on the planet, however, which was the only decent thing Kelly had ever done as far as I was concerned. Maisie had turned seven at Easter, and she was a constant delight. We'd bonded over a mutual love of fairy bread and my golden retriever, Rufus, and we were great pals now that I was going out with her dad.

Which made it all the more horrifying that Kelly was dragging Curtis back to court, trying to get full custody of Maisie so she could move her to Italy permanently. I hadn't even known Maisie a year, and I'd be devastated to lose the curly headed little monkey. How Curtis would stand the loss, I couldn't imagine.

"Is there any word on Curtis's case?" Heidi asked.

"The hearing's in ten days," I said. "I guess we'll finally have it resolved one way or the other then."

Heidi gave me a sympathetic smile. "It will be good to have it over with, whatever the outcome. The not knowing must be killing you."

"How is dear Curtis?" Aunt Evie asked.

"As well as you'd expect. Pretty stressed. He pretends he's confident when we talk about it, but I can tell he's worried."

Aunt Evie fired up in defence of her favourite policeman. "He shouldn't be. What judge in his right mind is going to let a woman like Kelly drag that sweet child to the other side of the world, away from her father and friends and everyone she's ever known?"

"Judges often favour the mother," Priya pointed out.

I nodded. "And Kelly's been putting on a good show lately. It's a long time since she got done for possession. She'll flutter those eyelashes and give the judge some sob story about wanting to show her daughter the world, and how she can't *bear* to be parted from her darling child."

"No one's forcing her to move to Rome," Heidi said.

"Maybe you'll get a female judge," Aunt Evie said. "That would upset her apple cart."

"Maybe." A girl could certainly dream.

Andrea looked at her watch. "Well, I'll have to head

off. Thanks for the drink, ladies, but I have an early start tomorrow."

"Me, too." Heidi stood up, hoisting her oversized bag. "I promised Dave I'd only stay half an hour. I'll walk you to your car."

We all said goodnight, and Andrea fixed me with a stern glance before they headed out. "Make sure you finish the book before Tuesday night."

I gave her a lazy wave. "Not making any promises."

"Andrea certainly takes book club seriously," Priya said when they'd gone. "Don't tell her, but I haven't read it, either."

Aunt Evie frowned. "Then how did you know about the suicide and the lovers?"

Priya gave her a smug grin. "Google is your friend."

I laughed and changed the subject. We chatted for a few more minutes. Priya offered to buy another round, but Aunt Evie started making noises about leaving, and my own thoughts were trending in that direction, too. I'd fed Rufus before I came out, but I knew he'd be waiting impatiently for me to come home. That dog loved to curl up next to me on the bed. He took his sleeping very seriously —as did I, for that matter. It had been a big week. And I was looking forward to snuggling into bed with a book.

Not *Madame Bovary*, though. Something with vampires and werewolves, probably.

Curtis was working tonight, so Rufus was my only option for cuddles. Between shift work and having Maisie part-time, I didn't see Curtis as much as I would have liked. He only stayed over if Maisie was with her mother.

Kelly would use anything as ammunition in her fight to steal Maisie away, and I wouldn't put it past her to accuse Curtis of neglecting his daughter in favour of his new girlfriend. We didn't want to give her any ammunition.

"Well, girls," Aunt Evie said, "it's time for this princess to turn into a pumpkin."

I stood up to give her a kiss on her perfumed cheek. "I think you must have read a different version of Cinderella than I did."

"Whatever. I'll see you on Tuesday night?"

"Of cour—"

The most blood-curdling scream cut the air, followed by a dreadful thud. We all glanced toward the foyer.

"What on earth was that?" Aunt Evie breathed.

Priya was already on the move, her reporter's nose sniffing out a story. I hurried after her, trailed by several people from the bar. Nothing looked amiss in the foyer, though the receptionist had come out from behind his desk and had one hand on the heavy glass door, ready to open it to the night.

"Did you hear that?" he asked uncertainly. "It came from outside."

"Of course we did." Priya pushed past him.

The whole gaggle of us flooded outside. The Metropole stood on a clifftop, and the sound of the waves below was much louder out here. An icy breeze swept in from the ocean, and my arms pebbled with cold, the thin fabric of my cardigan no match for winter's bite.

At first, I saw nothing. The circular driveway was empty of cars, and the night seemed serene until Priya's gasp caught my attention. Off to the left, in the shadows beyond the lights of the portico, a woman lay on the concrete in a spreading stain of red, her long blond hair fanned out in a bloodied halo.

Priya ran to her, fell to her knees, and leaned over, checking her for a pulse, but it didn't take a doctor to tell her efforts were in vain.

It was Krystal, and she was dead.

CHAPTER 2

SHE HAD FALLEN ON HER BACK, ARMS OUTSTRETCHED, A LOOK OF terror on her pretty face. Her eyes were open, staring straight up into the black sky. She'd landed in such a way that her beautiful red dress was pooled around her upper thighs, showing her long, bare legs.

Adrenaline flooded my body even as a tiny corner of my brain noted that she was only wearing one shoe, her bare foot incongruous, almost outrageous. Something told me that the perfectly groomed Krystal wasn't the kind of woman who would like to be seen in such an odd state of partial undress.

"Oh, goodness," Aunt Evie gasped. "Is she—?"

Priya got to her feet slowly, her face grim. "Yes."

Behind me, someone vomited into the garden near the door. It was the receptionist, looking very pale and sweaty.

Aunt Evie went straight into mother hen mode, probably grateful for something to do. "Are you all right, dear? Perhaps you should sit down."

He did look quite wobbly. He had one of those wispy moustaches that young men like to attempt before their facial hair is really up to the job. His voice cracked as he said, "I've never seen a dead body before."

I wished I could say the same, but this wasn't my first rodeo. "I'll call the police," I said to Priya. Someone needed to, and the poor receptionist didn't seem up to it. Aunt Evie was walking him back inside, guiding him to one of the comfortable lounges in the foyer. I pulled out my phone, noting the time as I did so. Five minutes after nine.

"We need a doctor," a man in the crowd said. "Somebody help her."

"Too late for that," Priya said. "Everybody stay back, please. The police will need to look at everything when they get here. They won't thank us for trampling all over their crime scene."

"What crime? Surely, she fell?"

I stepped away, leaving them all to crane their necks up at the balconies above us, trying to work out which one she'd fallen from. Though my heart was hammering against my ribs, my hands were surprisingly steady as I dialled the emergency number and waited to be connected to the police operator. I gave a quick report of the situation, and the operator assured me that someone would be with us within a few minutes.

I hung up and went to join Priya at the edge of the circular driveway. The bushes behind us rustled in the sharp ocean breeze, and I folded my arms tightly across my chest, trying to keep warm. A few of the onlookers had moved back into the relative warmth of the foyer, but most of the crowd was still here, awaiting the arrival of the police.

I scanned the area for Krystal's missing shoe, thinking that a bright red stiletto would be easy to spot, but there was no sign of it. It must have fallen into the garden. No doubt someone would find it in the morning.

"I wonder which one was her room?" Priya asked.

We both looked up at the façade of the hotel. The Metropole was a grand old lady, a little shabby in places, but her art deco charm was still strong. There were only three floors of guest rooms. Each room had a beautiful wrought iron balcony with ivy creeping across the stone walls in between. Perhaps half the rooms had lights on, and a few people had come out onto their balconies to gaze down at the tragedy unfolding below. I noted that the railings came up to chest height on the people leaning on them.

"*I* wonder how she could have fallen." None of the railings directly above us looked broken. "Those railings are quite high. Do you think she was sitting on it?"

"Could have been. But it's a cold night to be lounging around on balconies."

Blue and red lights flashed across the driveway, announcing the arrival of the police car. It pulled up under the portico, and a giant of a man got out, pulling his police cap down over his short, dark hair.

Priya threw me a wry grin. "I guess that's one way to see your boyfriend when he's working."

"Not one I would have chosen," I said, though I smiled at Curtis as he approached, his partner Delia at his side. The shaky feeling inside me settled, comforted by his presence.

His warm brown eyes ran over me, as if assuring himself I was unharmed. "Are you okay?" he asked in that deep voice I loved.

"I'm fine. But this poor lady ..." I indicated the body behind us. "Her name's Krystal Dendekker, and she's here for a conference. That's all I know."

Delia eyed the crowd gathered outside and those huddled in the foyer. "Are any of these people witnesses?"

"I don't think anyone saw her fall," I said. "We all came outside when we heard her scream."

Delia strode over to talk to the crowd, expertly shepherding them back inside as she did. Curtis crouched by the body, taking in every detail.

"Paramedics will be here soon," he said. "Not that they can do anything for her, the poor woman. The coroner will have to get involved."

He stood up, towering over Priya and I, but I didn't feel intimidated. It was a relief to have him here, so capable and reassuring. He gazed up and assessed the balconies for a long moment before taking out a notebook. "Tell me what happened."

Between the two of us, we got the story out quickly. There wasn't much to tell. Although ... I hesitated.

Curtis didn't miss it. "Was there something else?"

"I feel like I should mention ..."

"Go on."

"We did see her arguing with a man earlier. In the bar. She stormed out."

"And he left not long afterwards," Priya added.

"When was this?" Curtis asked.

I looked at Priya. "Maybe ten minutes before we heard her fall? Fifteen?"

"Do you know the man?"

I shrugged, and Priya said, "Never seen him before."

Curtis gestured with his pen at the crowd inside the foyer. "Is he here now?"

I ran my eye over the gathering, but most of them were locals having Friday night drinks, like us. A few strangers were probably hotel guests, but I didn't recognise any of them. I shook my head.

"I'll get you two to wait inside with the others, then," Curtis said, putting his notebook away as an ambulance roared up the driveway, lights flashing but siren silent. "It's too cold to be standing around out here. No one has touched the body, have they?"

"I checked for a pulse," Priya said, "but that's all."

Curtis nodded and went to talk to the paramedics.

Where was the man Krystal had been arguing with? Presumably, he was her partner, but he didn't work for the Kleins; he hadn't been present for the photo shoot this afternoon.

Thinking of the Kleins brought me up short as we went inside. All those people I'd met earlier in the day, Krystal's coworkers—none of them knew what had happened. One of them had mentioned a dinner at the hotel tonight, celebrating the firm making it through another gruelling year. They might be still partying, unaware that one of their own was sprawled on the cold concrete with the back of her skull smashed in.

Someone had to tell them what had happened.

"I'll be back in a minute," I said to Priya.

She nodded distractedly, still watching the tableau outside through the glass walls of the foyer. We might have been asked to leave the scene, but she was a reporter first and foremost. She could no more go home now than she could fly to the moon.

The Metropole was a small hotel. The ground floor had the bar and the main dining area, as well as office space and reception. The next floor up had conference rooms and function rooms, a small library and sitting area, as well as a smaller restaurant with a cheerful Italian theme. The final three floors had the guest rooms.

I headed up the grand, sweeping staircase to the first floor. If the staff of Klein's World of Kristmas had been in the main dining room, they probably would have heard the news already with all the people coming and going. My guess was that they were dining in La Cucina upstairs.

Of course, they might have already finished dinner and dispersed. Krystal and her partner had made their way to the bar earlier, after all. Perhaps they were all back in their rooms already. But some of them might have lingered over their coffee and tiramisu. I knew from firsthand experience that the tiramisu here was definitely worth lingering over.

I hurried into La Cucina, scanning the small room. No one from Klein's was here.

A smiling waiter came over. "Can I help you?"

"Did you have a booking here tonight under the name of Klein? Or Dendekker?" Krystal had probably organised it, so she might have made the booking in her own name.

The waiter didn't even need to consult the reservations book. "In the private room." He gestured toward a screen that separated the main part of the room from a smaller, more exclusive area. A burst of laughter came from there, as if on cue. "Some of them are still here."

"Oh, good." My feet were already moving across the patterned carpet. "I just need a quick word."

Five people were clustered around one end of a long table that had been set for eleven. I recognised all of them from our photo shoot this afternoon: old Mr Klein at the head and his wife at his right hand, plus two women and a man, who were all related to him in some way.

Mr Klein was telling some story that everyone found very amusing. He broke off at my entrance, smiling at me. "Ah, here's our intrepid photographer again! What brings you here, Charlie?" Then, to his wife, "Did I tell you this young lady found that stolen jewellery last year?"

Mrs Klein smiled at me. "Smart as well as pretty. Perhaps we should offer her a job, Robert."

The younger woman next to her, whose name had slipped my mind, cut in. "Is something wrong, Charlie?"

"I'm very sorry, but I have some terrible news."

"What, don't tell me there was no film in the camera," Mr Klein joked.

"Dad, no one uses film cameras anymore," the young woman said. She was the Kleins' daughter, and had inherited her mother's dark hair and green eyes, though her dress sense leaned more to the boho than her mother's conservative style. She wore a paisley shirt and had enough silver chains draped around her neck to start a jewellery shop. I couldn't remember what her role at the company was. Something to do with design?

Movement behind me announced the arrival of one of Mr Klein's sons. Adam? Andrew? I was usually better at remembering names, particularly when I'd spent some time photographing people and chatting to put them at ease, but shock had driven the details of the afternoon from my mind. He had the same receding hairline and stubborn jaw as his father, and carried a pale pink cardigan over one arm, which he offered to his wife as he sat down.

"No, it's not about the photos," I said. "It's about Krystal. There's been an accident." I paused. There was really no good way to say such a thing. "I'm afraid she's dead."

Mr Klein put a hand to his chest, and I had a sudden horrifying vision of him having a heart attack at the table and following Krystal into the afterlife. "Dead?"

His daughter had covered her mouth and was staring at me in wide-eyed shock. Silence reigned for an agonised moment.

"What happened?" the son asked, pausing in the act of helping his wife into her cardigan.

"She fell from her balcony. The police are outside with her now. I think you had better come."

CHAPTER 3

<small>THE LIFT WAS SILENT AS WE RODE DOWNSTAIRS TOGETHER.</small> MRS Klein clutched her husband's arm. Their son—Angus, that was his name—had his arm around his pretty blond wife, his jaw set in a grim line. Everyone's face was pale, shock and grief in their eyes.

"Feeling warmer, darling?" Angus murmured to his wife.

She nodded. "If I'd known how cold it would be in that restaurant, I would have worn something else." She gave me a tremulous smile. "I had to send poor Angus back to our room to get me a cardigan before I froze to death. He's so good to me."

When we got downstairs, more police had arrived and were taking photos of the body. Upon seeing Krystal, Mrs Klein gave a tortured little squeak and started to cry. The balding guy next to her, who I seemed to remember was a nephew, pulled a handkerchief from his pocket and handed it to her.

"Where's Justin?" Mr Klein asked.

"That poor boy," Mrs Klein whispered into the hanky. Hanky guy patted her awkwardly on the back.

"Is Justin her husband?" I asked. If he was the guy from the bar, I'd very much like to know where he was, too, though perhaps for different reasons than the Kleins. Mr Klein nodded, still staring at the scene outside. I put my hand on his arm. "Perhaps you should all wait here a moment while I go get the police to come and talk to you."

He nodded distractedly, and I hurried out into the cold night air again. Priya and Aunt Evie followed me out a moment later.

"Are those the people from the Christmas company?" Aunt Evie asked. Priya looked back at them curiously.

"Yeah. One of them probably needs to formally ID the body. I'll go talk to Curtis."

But I'd barely taken two steps when a shout rang out.

"That's my wife!" The man we'd seen arguing with Krystal in the bar—Justin—had just sprinted up the driveway, his vibrant flamingo shirt partially hidden under a heavy jacket. He fell to his knees by the body. "What's happened? Don't just stand there, help her!"

Curtis caught him by the shoulders when he reached out to gather Krystal into his arms. "Sir, I'm very sorry, but your wife is dead. Please don't touch her until the coroner arrives."

"The coroner?" The man stared up at Curtis in confusion. "No, she's just ... She needs to go to hospital." He shrugged Curtis's hand off in a violent motion and bounced to his feet again. "You have to take her to hospital."

One of the paramedics, an older woman, took his arm. "Come and sit down over here, love."

"I don't want to sit." He slapped the woman's hand away, shouting in her face. "Just do your job. You have to do your job!"

Curtis moved in. "Sir, take a deep breath, please."

"Don't tell me what to do!" He flung his hands out, spun around, and almost walked into the side of the ambulance.

Curtis hovered, but the fight seemed to go out of Justin. All at once, he was leaning against the vehicle, sobbing like a baby. When the paramedic approached him again, he offered no resistance. She guided him toward the back of the ambulance, where she wrapped a blanket around his shoulders and urged him to sit. He bent over, elbows on knees, and buried his face in his hands.

"That's him," I said to Curtis in a low voice. "The guy we saw arguing with her earlier."

Delia eyed him thoughtfully, then went and crouched in front of him. "Sir, can I ask you a few questions?"

He nodded without removing his hands from his face.

"What's your name?"

"Justin Dendekker." His voice was muffled, tearful.

"And your wife's name?"

"Krystal. Krystal Dendekker."

"It appears your wife fell from the balcony. Are you staying at the hotel?"

Justin nodded again.

"Which one is your room?"

He lifted his face and looked up at the hotel's façade. His eyes and nose were red, his cheeks streaked with tears. He indicated a dark balcony on the top floor. "That one. Or maybe that one." His finger wavered between two. "I can't tell from here. It's room 428."

I looked up, wondering if they'd been one room over whether the roof of the portico might have broken her fall. Whether she might have lived. But there was nothing except concrete driveway and a little edging of garden below the Dendekkers' room.

"Can you tell me about your wife's movements tonight?" Delia asked.

A frown crinkled Justin's ravaged face. "Her movements?"

She nodded reassuringly. "Did you have dinner together? When did she go to the room? Was she alone there?"

"I ..." He rubbed the back of his neck and looked back up at the balconies overhead. Then he turned a look of deep suspicion on Delia, some of his fight returning. "Why are you asking me that?"

Delia was unruffled. It struck me that her position, crouched so that she was lower than him, was deliberately unthreatening. "It's just procedure for any accidental death. We have to try to establish what happened, to help the coroner. We'll be talking to lots of people." She gave him a moment to process that. He seemed slow on the uptake, and I wondered how much he'd had to drink before the two of them left the bar. "When did you last see your wife alive?"

"I don't know." He clutched his head as if it hurt to think, burying his fingers in his hair. "Not that long ago. Maybe half an hour. We were just in the bar after dinner, and we ... we had a bit of a disagreement. So she went to the room, and I went out for a walk on the beach. Just to clear my head."

"I see. And what was this disagreement about?"

He waved a hand, and I noticed it was shaking. "Nothing. Nothing serious. Just stupid stuff, like all married couples do. I don't even remember."

Priya glanced at me, one eyebrow raised. It certainly hadn't looked like *nothing* to us. The way his hand had closed on her arm, fingers digging into her flesh. That had looked like it would leave a bruise.

"How long were you gone, would you say?"

Justin looked up at the night sky, as if the answer were written in the stars. "Not long. It was cold out, and I was tired. I thought I'd get an early night. Then I came up the driveway and saw the cop car, and all the people ... and Krystal ..." He dashed a hand across his eyes, wiping away a fresh flood of tears. "How could she have fallen?"

He surged up, almost knocking Delia over with the suddenness of the movement. "*How could she have fallen?*" he shouted. "The balcony must be faulty. I'm going to sue these people for everything they've got! Where's the manager?"

He started for the front doors, his hair sticking out every which way, a wild look in his eyes. Curtis moved to stop him, and Delia hurried behind like a sheepdog nipping at Justin's heels.

Mr Klein burst out of the hotel, trailed by the other members of his family. "What's going on?" he demanded.

Behind us, a car door slammed.

"Oh, look," said Priya. "Your number one fan is here."

The tall, rumpled, and perpetually grumpy figure of Detective McGovern strode over to join the group milling near the doors. Detective McGovern didn't approve of amateurs "sticking their noses into police investigations" as he called it, even if I had helped solve a few of his cases recently. We hadn't clashed since last year, so he might have gotten over his dislike of me, but I moved behind Priya anyway, hoping he wouldn't notice me.

No such luck. His eyes narrowed when he caught sight of me. I guess I still wasn't his favourite person, then. But he couldn't complain about me interfering. All I'd done was stand here. Technically, it was Priya who had discovered the body.

Fortunately for me, right now his focus was on Justin, who was now held firmly in Curtis's strong grip.

"Who are all these people?" McGovern spared a glance for the Kleins and other bystanders, then gestured to Delia. "This isn't a show. Get everyone inside and start taking statements."

Mr Klein drew himself up. "The young lady worked for us. She's been my personal assistant for almost six years."

His lip quivered, and even McGovern's irritated look softened.

"I'm sorry for your loss, folks, but I'll ask you to step

inside for now. There's nothing you can do out here. You, too." His gaze included Priya, Aunt Evie, and me.

"Now, just hold on a minute there, son," Mr Klein protested.

Mrs Klein plucked at his sleeve. "Robert, perhaps we should—"

Delia stepped smoothly in before McGovern could say anything. "Right this way, ladies and gents. I'm sure this is a terrible shock for all of you." She kept talking as she made shepherding motions with her hands, gradually getting them moving back through the doors. Aunt Evie, Priya, and I lingered.

McGovern turned to Curtis. "Who is this?"

"The deceased's husband, Justin Dendekker," Curtis said, releasing Justin as he spoke.

"My condolences," McGovern said as Justin adjusted his sleeves and brushed at his arms, as if he could brush away Curtis's touch. "Are you able to answer a few questions now, Mr Dendekker?"

"I already told the policewoman everything," Justin said, giving him a sour glance. "Who are you?"

McGovern reached into his jacket and pulled out a card. "Detective Luke McGovern. Was your wife drinking tonight?"

"She probably had a couple." His eyes had a vacant look about them as they flitted about, never resting long on anything. "Nothing wrong with that."

"Of course not," McGovern said soothingly. "Just trying to establish the facts. And were you with your wife when she fell?"

Justin glowered at him. "No."

"Where were you?"

"Like I *said* to the policewoman, walking on the beach."

"Has your wife been acting at all differently lately?"

"What do you mean, differently?"

"Has she seemed upset or withdrawn?"

Justin frowned. "Are you trying to say she jumped? That she did this on *purpose*?" His voice got louder as his outrage grew. "Krystal would never do that. She fell. Maybe she was a little tipsy, but she would never *jump*. She *fell*."

Detective McGovern exchanged glances with Curtis, who stepped in to calm Justin again. "Just following procedure, sir. We have to consider all the possibilities."

"Really?" Priya muttered to me. "*All* of them? Including that she might have been pushed?"

"Surely not by him." Aunt Evie indicated Justin with a movement of her head. "Not if he was on the beach."

Priya contemplated the grieving husband. "I wonder if anyone can confirm that alibi?"

Aunt Evie snorted. "Keep talking like that and Detective McGovern will take a dislike to you, too."

"Oh, he already dislikes me. The police think of the press as a necessary evil. Now ask me if I care."

I folded my arms, fighting the urge to shiver. It was freezing out here. Detective McGovern's breath formed little puffs of white in the dark air as he talked to Justin. "We'll have to see your room," he was saying.

Justin nodded sulkily and pulled a keycard from his

pocket, offering it to the detective. They headed inside, leaving Curtis to secure the scene. He shooed us inside, and I was glad to go. I could barely feel my toes anymore.

"That poor man," Aunt Evie said, watching Justin waiting by the lifts with McGovern.

"He might need a sedative," Priya murmured. "He's taking it pretty hard."

"Mmm." I nodded agreement, contemplating the grieving man's shoes. They were buffed to a high shine, and had not a speck of dirt or sand on them.

Pretty strange, considering he said he'd been walking on the beach.

CHAPTER 4

THE LIFT DOORS CLOSED ON JUSTIN AND THE DETECTIVE, AND Aunt Evie sprang into action. She went over to talk to the receptionist, who was back behind the desk but still looked pale. I heard her mention blankets.

"I'm sure you could all do with a nice cup of tea," she said when she came back to the Klein family. They were standing by the doors, looking lost. "Why don't we all sit down over here?" She shepherded them toward a vacant pair of lounges.

"I'll go and see about that tea," Priya said, heading for the bar.

"I'll help you," I said, glad for something useful to do.

The bartender was happy to make tea, though grilled us for information the whole time he was working. We told him what we knew, which wasn't much. When we came back into the foyer with a tray of teacups each, Aunt Evie was handing out blankets, and Delia had pulled a chair over to the group and was writing in her notebook.

"And how do you all know Krystal?" she was asking as we entered.

"She works for us," Mr Klein said. "She's my personal assistant."

Delia looked around the group. "Do you all work together?"

I passed out cups of tea as the conversation continued around me.

"Yes. This is my wife Susan and my daughter Stephanie." Mr Klein indicated the two ladies as he spoke.

"I'm not very involved with the business anymore," Mrs Klein said almost apologetically. Though she had a sleek, dark bob, her face looked almost as wrinkled as Aunt Evie's. I was guessing she'd had her children quite late. "Stephanie has taken over as our designer."

Stephanie gave Delia a little wave. Her legs were crossed, showing the most amazing pair of cowboy boots peeking out from under her full skirt. Her style was certainly eclectic.

Mr Klein continued impatiently with the introductions. "My son Angus and his wife Delphine, and my nephew Donal."

There was a subdued chorus of hellos around the circle. Angus was a slightly taller version of his father, with darker hair and less of a beer gut. His wife was blond, pretty, and delicate, though perhaps sitting next to her beefy husband contributed to that impression.

"Angus is the head of our construction team," Mrs Klein said.

I blinked. What sort of Christmas decorations were

these people making? *Head of construction* made me think of earthmoving equipment and trucks full of cement.

"And Donal is our accountant," her daughter Stephanie added helpfully. "He's a whiz with numbers."

"That's me," Donal said awkwardly. He was the guy who'd offered his hanky to Mrs Klein. He looked exactly how I imagined an accountant should look: balding, a bit earnest, with dark-rimmed glasses.

Delia made notes in her book, then looked up at Mr Klein. "And you are—?"

Mr Klein puffed out his chest ever so slightly. "Robert Klein, head of Klein's World of Kristmas. We supply decorations to shopping centres and corporate facilities. Best in the business."

I noted Delia didn't write that down. "I see," she said. "And why were you all here tonight?"

"Today was our annual planning meeting," Mr Klein said. "I'm retiring soon, and we've been discussing what the future looks like once my boy Travis steps into the CEO position."

"We rented a conference room in the hotel," Stephanie said. "And Dad sprang for dinner and hotel rooms for everyone for the weekend so we could make a celebration of it."

"Was Krystal at dinner with you?"

"Yes."

"And her husband, Justin? Anyone else?"

"Our other son, Travis," Mrs Klein said. "His wife Yumi and their boy Brandon."

Brandon, I recalled, had been a very reluctant participant in the family photo this afternoon, a surly teen scowling at the camera.

"It was a celebration of Travis's promotion," Mr Klein added.

"Where are they now?"

"In their rooms," Mrs Klein said. "Travis had to make some calls. We should tell them, Robert."

Mr Klein patted her knee. "Let's finish up here first."

She nodded and took a sip of her tea.

"Do you know where Krystal and Justin went when they left dinner?" Delia asked.

"I think they were going back to their room, too," Stephanie said. "Krystal had a headache."

"Did Krystal have much to drink at dinner?"

"A glass or two?" Stephanie looked around the group uncertainly.

"No, she didn't have any," Delphine interjected. "She's just started that new diet, remember? No alcohol."

I watched Delia write *no alcohol* in her notepad. Without looking up, she asked, "How long has she been on this diet?"

"Almost two weeks," Delphine said. "If it was me, I would have waited until after this weekend. I told her as much, too. But that was Krystal. She always knew best."

"She's a very confident young woman," Mr Klein said. "Was. She *was* a confident young woman." Mrs Klein covered his hand with her own as he paused to clear his throat. He turned his hand to clasp hers, and I wondered if Curtis and I would ever be an old married couple finding simple comfort in each other's touch. "She was a real asset to the business. She always seemed to know what I needed without being told. I couldn't have asked for a better assistant."

Delia asked something else, but my mind had wandered off. Surely, Krystal's husband would have known she was off alcohol? So why would he suggest she might have fallen because she was drunk?

Admittedly, they hadn't seemed to be on the best of terms when I saw them arguing at the bar. Maybe they didn't talk much. Or perhaps he *had* known, but the shock of seeing her dead had driven it from his mind. I always liked to give people the benefit of the doubt.

Aunt Evie yawned, covering her mouth with one ring-heavy hand. We were hovering awkwardly off to one side with Priya, having finished handing out blankets and cups of tea.

"I should head home," she said. "It's past my bedtime, and you know how I am if I don't get my beauty sleep."

I nodded. "Monstrous."

She pretended to be outraged. "How can you say such a thing to your beloved aunt?"

I smiled. "Because it's true?"

Aunt Evie was one of those horrendously chipper morning people, but only if she'd gotten her full eight hours of sleep.

"I don't think there's much else we can do here," Priya said. "I saw a suit go outside a moment ago. Looked like hotel management. I'm going to see if McGovern will give me a statement for the paper, then I might call it a night, too."

"If I'd known your Friday night drinks were this eventful, I would have been too afraid to come," Aunt Evie said as she gave Priya a farewell peck on the cheek.

I walked Aunt Evie to her car, which was thankfully parked near mine in the guest carpark out back, so we didn't have to incur Detective McGovern's wrath by trampling through his crime scene again. Where the grumpy detective was concerned, I was all for keeping a low profile. It was painful to be so thoroughly disliked by someone when all I'd tried to do was be helpful, and I was *more* than happy to leave him to handle poor Krystal's death on his own. It was his job, after all, and despite what he seemed to think, I wasn't the least bit interested in taking it over or showing him up.

Home was a cozy little duplex only a couple of minutes away, and I was glad to pull into my driveway. I knew a certain dog who would be very happy to see me.

On the other side of the row of bushes that separated my driveway from the one next door, my neighbour Jack was pulling his bag out of his back seat. I parked my little Mazda in the garage, then came out to say hello. Between his shift work and my somewhat erratic schedule, I didn't get to see him as often as I would have liked.

He was still wearing his blue nurse's scrubs, and there were tired circles under his eyes. He kept his beard trimmed neatly, but his curly dark hair was getting long enough to flop all over the place, and he brushed it out of his face impatiently.

"Hi, there," I said over the bushes. "Did you have the afternoon shift today?"

"Yep." He straightened up and slammed the car door. "Rose called in sick, so we were run off our feet. How are you?"

"Fine, I guess."

He paused, giving me an assessing glance. "Only fine? Bad day at work?"

"No. I've just come from the Metropole. I was having drinks with the girls, and some poor woman fell from her balcony."

His eyes widened. "Is she—?"

"Yep. She fell from the top floor onto the concrete."

He winced. "That's nasty."

I nodded, remembering the spreading pool of blood beneath Krystal's body. "Yeah. She didn't stand a chance."

"Are you okay? Do you want to come in?"

He was such a sweetheart. It was a pity he wasn't *really* Priya's boyfriend.

"No, thanks, I'm good. Besides, Rufus would think it was the worst kind of betrayal. I'm sure he's heard I'm home by now."

"He could come, too." Jack loved that dog almost as much as I did.

"It's fine," I said. "I just can't help thinking ... that poor woman. One minute she's sitting there in the bar, the next she's dead on the driveway. So sudden."

"You saw her in the bar?"

"Yeah. She was arguing with her husband, actually. Then she storms out, he follows. Ten minutes later it's all over, red rover."

Jack's eyebrows rose. "You think he killed her?"

37

"Does that make me a terrible person? It was the first thing I thought when I saw her. And then he comes back *from a walk*"—I made quotation marks in the air with my fingers—"and says she was probably drunk and fell. Only, wouldn't you think her own husband would know she'd given up drinking the week before? It was like he was trying to explain it away as an accident."

Jack shrugged. "Accidents do happen."

"I know, but wouldn't it be hard to fall off a balcony if you were sober?"

"You'd think so, but I've seen people do all kinds of stupid things. You wouldn't believe some of the things I saw when I worked in Emergency in Brisbane. I had one kid who'd been trying to jump from one balcony to the next at a party. That didn't end well for him."

"But she wasn't a kid. And she wasn't drinking."

"You can't be sure of that. The drinking, I mean. Why would her husband suggest it if she actually *had* given up drinking? He must have realised it would make him look dodgy. Who told you she'd given up?"

"One of the women she worked with."

"Well, she wouldn't be the first to fall off the wagon. Or off a balcony, for that matter. The police toxicology report will sort it all out." He hefted his backpack over one shoulder. "You don't need to worry about it, unless ... You're not thinking of getting involved again, are you?"

I shuddered. "Heavens, no. Never again."

Famous last words.

CHAPTER 5

S ATURDAY DAWNED BRIGHT AND CLEAR. I T WAS A BEAUTIFUL DAY
for a walk, so Rufus and I headed out early. Even though it
was the middle of winter and the wind off the ocean was
biting, the sun still gave a little warmth. Besides, Rufus
had his fur coat and I had a warm jacket zipped up right to
my chin and a beanie pulled down over my ears.

Down on the beach, Rufus found some seagulls, which
thrilled him very much. The seagulls were less impressed.
They lifted into the air almost huffily every time he got
close, wobbling in the wind and clearly resenting the
necessity. Once he'd moved past, they settled on the sand
again, casting reproachful glances at me as if to say *can't
you keep your beast under better control?* But I was in no
mood to repress Rufus's energy. Watching him lope along
the beach, tongue hanging out one side of his mouth in a
lopsided doggy grin, made me happy. And after the night
before, I was all in favour of happy.

I was still thinking about Krystal and her unfortunate

end when Rufus took off ahead, following some smell or other up the steep steps from the beach and along the grassy verge of the road above. I had no particular place to be this morning, so I let him lead me up the hill toward the Metropole, following his nose. Not that I was in any great hurry to revisit the scene of the crime, but there was a lovely nature walk along the cliff up there, with gorgeous views back across the bay, and a bit of nature would cheer my soul.

I glanced up the long driveway of the hotel as we passed. There was no sign that a woman had lost her life only hours before. As far as I could tell at this distance, the concrete where she'd landed was clean. There wasn't even any police tape. I supposed there wasn't much point in the police lingering. She was dead, and if it was because of foul play, there wouldn't be any clues as to who had killed her on the driveway. It was far more likely that room 428 would hold the answers to the police's questions. If indeed there were any answers to be found.

Rufus trotted further along the road to where the houses ended and the bush began, untroubled by thoughts of murder and justice. The local council had created a walking track here with steps at the steepest parts, and even a small boardwalk over a particularly marshy section further on. The track wound around the edge of the cliff, offering views in both directions and out to sea. Later in the year, it was a good place to watch for whales migrating up the east coast of Australia, but this morning, there was no one here but a man walking with his young son. The kid looked about nine or ten, but he wasn't too old to make a big fuss over Rufus.

"Can I pat him?" the boy asked as Rufus trotted over, tail wagging, ready to accept any offerings of love or food.

"Go ahead," I said. "He's friendly."

Rufus proved my point by licking the boy's nose as he bent down, which made him squeal and laugh.

"Looks like you won't need a shower this morning," the boy's father said as the kid rewarded Rufus with many pats.

We said goodbye and walked on. The beach was definitely Rufus's favourite place to roam, but this clifftop walk came a close second. There were so many good smells to sniff, lizards to chase under bushes, and birds to bark at. In short, everything to keep a dog happily occupied for hours at a time.

The wind was cooler up here, so I pulled my jacket more tightly around my neck, wishing I had thought to bring a scarf. The wind ruffled Rufus's fur, but he didn't seem to mind. He trotted ahead of me, tail held high like a furry flag. We crossed the boardwalk, my steps echoing hollowly on the planks, and got back on the track, where the decomposing leaves and pine needles muffled the sound of my feet again. Something small scuttled in the leaves, and Rufus dived under a bush in hot pursuit.

"Leave it, Rufus." He was the bane of all the lizards who tried to live in my little backyard. More than once, I'd gone to hang out my washing and discovered half a lizard carcass in the grass.

Rufus's tail wagged, but otherwise, he took no notice

of me. Eventually, he gave up on his hunt and backed out of the bush, fortunately minus lizard. A little further on, he found some compelling scent under the trees and shoved his face into the undergrowth again.

"One of these days, you're going to find a snake, doing things like that," I warned him. "And I don't know which of you will be more horrified."

His tail moved gently at the sound of my voice. I kept walking, knowing that he would catch up. It was too cold to stand around doing nothing.

When he caught up with me, he had something in his mouth. For a horrified second, I thought it was some small animal covered in blood, but a closer look revealed that it was only a shoe. He trotted up to me with the jaunty air of a hero who has slain the dragon and dropped it at my feet.

"Good boy," I said, since he seemed to expect praise for his mighty deed, though my heart began to pound as I bent to pick it up. "Where on earth did you find that?"

The shoe looked reasonably fresh, as if it hadn't spent very long outside. Apart from a couple of indentations from Rufus's teeth, a few strands of grass, and a whole lot of dog slobber, there weren't any other marks. It was also horribly familiar.

Suddenly, I was back on the floodlit cement of the Metropole's grand circular driveway, gazing down at a body in a red dress. I saw Priya checking for a pulse that wasn't there.

And I saw Krystal's long, tanned legs outstretched. One of them terminated in an elegant red stiletto. The other, a cold, pale foot with toenails painted a dark purple.

"Oh, no." I stared down at the shoe in my hand. Should I drop it? I knew I shouldn't be touching it. It was evidence, and there might be fingerprints or some kind of DNA on it. Should I put it back where it had been? But I didn't even know where that was.

If only real life were like the movies. Lassie would have confidently led someone right to the spot, where some other clue would have conveniently identified the person who had left it there. Rufus, on the other hand, gazed lovingly up at me and beat his long, plumed tail gently against the earth behind him, stirring up bits of dirt and leaves. There was no way he would run back and assume a pointer stance, miraculously revealing the hiding place of the shoe and solving the case in one blow.

I walked slowly back a few paces along the trail anyway, examining the undergrowth on the side where Rufus had been rooting around. But if there was some sign there, I missed it. Nothing looked out of place. No one had helpfully dropped their name badge at the same time as they hid the shoe. I snorted to myself. If only it were that easy.

"But how did this get here?" I asked the dog. His ears twitched at the sound of my voice. Something wasn't adding up.

Krystal had been wearing the mate to this shoe when she died. And considering the height of the heel, she wouldn't have been walking around with only one on. So why was this one here? *How* had it got here? I turned it slowly in my hand, trying not to move my fingers. I'd already contaminated whatever evidence the shoe may have been able to give us. Detective McGovern wouldn't thank me for making the situation worse by pawing the whole thing.

The only way this could have got here—no, the only *person* who could have put it here—was the murderer. But why? What was so incriminating about this one shoe that they had to run and hide it under some random bushes so that it could never be found?

I thought again of Justin—appearing out of the night, horrified to find his wife dead on the driveway. Had he really been walking on the beach? Or had he come here to hide this apparently vital piece of evidence?

I shook my head. It didn't make sense. If the shoe had fallen on the balcony when the murderer pushed her over, why not just leave it there? It wasn't as if it was the only thing they could have left their DNA on. It was probably all over her body. "Come on, boy. We'd better give this to Detective McGovern."

We headed back down the hill. The police station was in Waterloo Bay, the next town over, so I left Rufus in the backyard, tucked the shoe into a plastic shopping bag, and drove over there. Maybe Detective McGovern wouldn't be working today. It was Saturday, after all. Did detectives get the weekend off?

I sighed as I found a parking spot not far from the police station. They probably worked shift work, the same as Curtis did. And it was even more probable that they worked the morning after they got a big new case. I headed into the police station with nerves fluttering in the pit of my stomach like butterflies. It would be so much easier if I could just hand my bag over to the desk sergeant.

Alas, the stars did not align. Not only was Detective McGovern working today, but I could see him at his desk as soon as I walked in. The public part of the foyer was separated from the rest of the station by a long counter with protective glass screens, but the working part of the police station remained visible. I didn't even have to speak to the smiling woman behind the desk. McGovern looked up as if he had some sixth sense that warned him when the annoying local photographer appeared, scowled, and marched straight over to the window to greet me.

"Yes, Miss Carter? Can I help you?"

Well, he wasn't winning any community relations awards with that approach. His tone was short and begrudging and there was no welcome at all in his tired face.

"Hi," I said with enough brightness to light a football stadium, as if my cheeriness could make up for his grouchy approach. "I was out on a walk this morning with my dog, and he found something." I offered the plastic bag, and he took it as if it might contain a ticking bomb.

His frown deepened when he saw what was inside. "Where did you find this?" He took three swift steps back to his desk and pulled a pair of plastic gloves out of the top drawer, pulling them on before reaching into the bag.

"Up on the southern headland," I said. "On the trail around the cliffs, just past the boardwalk. It was hidden in the bushes."

He had pulled the shoe from the bag and was turning

it in his hand, carefully inspecting it. He shot me an unforgiving look. "And I suppose you just picked it up? Why is it wet here?"

I squared my shoulders against the hostility in his voice. "Yes, I touched it, but only after my dog had carried it in his mouth. That's what the wetness is—dog slobber."

His expression tightened. "Can you show me exactly where it was?"

"Not *exactly*. I can take you close, but I wasn't watching what Rufus was doing, so I'm not sure of the exact spot."

He sighed. "You should have left it so we could do a proper sweep of the area."

I lifted my chin, determined not to feel guilty for things that were out of my control. Although perhaps this was not the time to tell him I had poked around in the bushes myself in search of any other clues. "Well, I'm sorry, but I did the best I could. Rufus grabbed it, and I took it off him and brought it straight here. At least there's one good thing."

He sighed again. "And what's that?"

"Now we know she didn't fall by accident. Somebody killed her and tried to cover it up."

CHAPTER 6

I<small>T STARTED TO RAIN THAT AFTERNOON</small>, <small>BIG FAT DROPS THAT</small> drummed insistently on the roof and splattered against the windows. The weather could change fast here in Sunrise Bay, with storms rolling in from the ocean at a moment's notice. I sat at the dining table with Rufus curled up at my feet and worked on the photos I'd taken for Klein's World of Kristmas yesterday.

There were head shots of Mr Klein, his two sons, and his daughter. Krystal had told me that she was making a promotional brochure for their clients, featuring the heads of department. You could definitely tell they were related. There was something about the eyes.

Angus was the most like his father, both solid men of middling height, their muscle now starting to run to fat. Old Mr Klein had shrunk a little with age, but Angus's darker hair was receding in the exact same pattern as his father's, and they both had that stubborn square jaw.

Travis, the younger son, was taller than both of them,

I'd noticed. He also still had a full head of hair, unlike his brother and father. It was dark and swept back from his forehead like an old-time movie star's. He was also in better shape, more of a slim build like his mother and Stephanie. He'd cracked jokes the whole time I'd been photographing him, and some of that laughter still lingered in his eyes in the photos.

Stephanie had definitely inherited her mother's genes, with that wavy dark hair and striking green eyes. She still had an element of that boho chic I'd seen last night in her workwear, which was a shapeless denim dress paired with a pretty floral scarf. That dress would have looked like a sack on me, but somehow, she managed to make it look effortlessly stylish.

Once I had finished with the individual shots, I moved on to the group photos. One set of photos was staff only and the other was family. Mostly, these featured the same people. As Mr Klein was fond of saying, Klein's was a family-oriented company.

For the staff photo, Mr Klein was front and centre, beaming from his seat in the middle of the front row. Stephanie sat on his right, and Krystal was on his left. The three younger Klein men stood behind them, with Travis, the heir apparent, in the middle. They were all smiling. The light had caught on Donal's glasses, so I spent some time fixing that up. Actually, he wasn't a Klein, was he? I'd forgotten his last name, but I remembered it was something different.

In the next photo, Mrs Klein took Krystal's place beside her husband, and another chair had been brought over and placed next to her. There had been some rearranging so that husbands stood behind their wives. Travis stood behind a very attractive woman who looked Chinese or Korean. I remembered she had an unusual name, though it took me a moment to recall it—Yumi. Next to him stood a surly teenage boy with Yumi's dark hair and eyes. I'd done my best, but I hadn't been able to wring a smile out of him. Angus was behind the cardigan-wearing Delphine, of course, and that left Donal to stand behind Stephanie. Either they were both single or their significant others had decided a whole weekend of talking about Klein's World of Kristmas wasn't their idea of a good time.

As always, it was a little tricky to get a perfect shot of that many people, and I had to do some creative photo-shopping. Delphine kept blinking at the wrong time, and I had to take the only decent shot of her and drop it into the best photo of the others. Donal's glasses were also problematic, but I removed the glare on the lenses and once I'd adjusted the lighting and contrast, I had something I was satisfied with. Since there were no photos where Travis's son deigned to smile, I had to settle for "brooding and beautiful" instead of "happy" where he was concerned.

I changed tabs and gazed at the staff photo, caught by Krystal's smile. Her beautiful, long hair was up in a stylish bun instead of the way I'd last seen it—splayed around her broken body. She wore a grey pin-striped pants suit and a soft pink blouse that matched her lipstick. She looked elegant and professional.

I searched her eyes for any hint of trouble. Justin had seemed angry in the bar, but could he really have become so enraged he killed her on a whim? Surely, her murder hadn't been a spur-of-the-moment thing? There must be more to it. Had she been aware that her time on this earth was ticking away? That some problem in her life was about to explode into disaster?

If she was aware of the doom hurtling to meet her, she gave no sign in this photo, smiling broadly for the camera. She was the only senior staff member who wasn't a relative, but she seemed perfectly comfortable there in the bosom of the Klein family. I had no photos of Justin, since he didn't work for them.

I sighed. "I wish we hadn't found that shoe, boy. It was better when I could hope that her death was an accident."

Curled up by my feet, Rufus thumped his tail on the floor but didn't bother opening his eyes.

I got up to stretch after sitting bent over my laptop for so long. That got more of a reaction from him. He lifted his head hopefully, perhaps wondering if there was another walk in the offing.

"I'm only going to the kitchen," I said. "I'm making coffee."

Of course, I could walk down to the surf club. The cafe there made really good coffee, far better than the stuff from my own kitchen. But I wanted to get this job finished before I headed out for dinner at Curtis's house tonight, so homemade coffee it was.

My phone rang while I was pottering about the kitchen.

"Hi," Priya said. "How's Sunny Bay's favourite sleuth?"

"What's that supposed to mean? I'll have you know

I'm sitting here minding my own business, working on a job for a client. No sleuthing going on here at all."

Her voice had an arch tinge to it. "That's not what I heard. A little birdie just told me that a certain someone found the missing shoe belonging to our victim from last night."

I put her on speaker and set the phone down on the bench so I could ladle sugar into my favourite cup. "That was completely accidental. I've sworn off any kind of sleuthing. Detective McGovern will kill me if I get involved again."

She made a derisive noise. "McGovern McShovern. It's a sign from the universe, Charlie. You were the one who found the shoe. It's meant to be."

"Actually, it was Rufus who found it, so by that logic, *he* should take over the investigation." I stirred the coffee and inhaled its blissful scent. "Word gets around fast. Who told you, anyway?"

I could hear the smugness in her voice. "I'm a news-paper reporter. I hear everything—it's my job. So, spill! Where was it? In the garden under the balcony? I thought the police looked there."

Her sources weren't as good as she thought, then. She had no idea. "They did look there. But it wasn't anywhere near the hotel. Rufus found it under a bush on the clifftop walk up on the headland."

"Seriously?" Nothing excited our intrepid reporter more than a whiff of intrigue. "It must be murder, then."

"That's what I thought, too." I added a generous dash

of milk to my coffee, then slammed the fridge door and carried my cup back into the dining room.

Priya went on, thinking out loud. "It must've fallen off when he pushed her over, so then he pretends to go for a walk on the beach but *actually* goes and stashes it in the bushes where he hopes no one will ever find it. I wonder why he didn't just chuck it in the bin at the hotel? Hmmm. Maybe he was worried the police would search those. Okay, so he goes for a walk to get rid of the evidence, then comes back and is all, *Oh no! she's dead.*"

"If by *he* you mean Justin, I did notice there wasn't any sand on his shoes last night, which seemed a little odd for someone who said he'd been walking on the beach."

"Exactly! That just proves he's our man."

I sat back in my chair, petting the patient Rufus with my foot. "But why bother to hide the shoe at all? Why not leave it on the balcony? How does that look incriminating? If she had fallen by accident, her shoe could have slipped off as she fell. The very act of hiding it makes it clear it was no accident. If he'd just left it alone, the police might've believed it was just a tragic slip, but now they know it was a murder. He's shot himself in the foot."

There was a pregnant pause on the other end of the line before Priya grudgingly admitted I was right.

"I still say he looks guilty, though," she added. "He probably just panicked. I mean, we saw them arguing in the bar just a few moments before she died. That doesn't give anyone else much time to do it, does it?"

"Maybe." It certainly looked bad for Justin, but I was always one to try and see both sides of any story. "It must have been at least ten minutes between when they both stormed out and when she fell, though. Remember, we chatted for a while, and then Heidi and Andrea left. And it wasn't straight after that, either. It could have been as much as fifteen minutes." I couldn't be sure now. The drama of the subsequent events had rather muddied the timeline in my head.

"Maybe." Priya didn't sound convinced. "But we both know in any murder, the husband or partner is the first person the police look at. And they're usually right."

I sighed. "The whole thing is so sad. I've just been looking at the photos I took of them all that afternoon. I can't believe everything could change so quickly."

"Was Justin in the photos?"

"No. He doesn't work for Klein's."

"Well, he has no alibi, so I still say he's the most likely suspect. The others were all together when you went to tell them that she was dead, weren't they? So none of them could have done it."

I cast my eye over the family photo again, with all the players sitting there smiling so nicely at the camera. Except that kid, of course. No power on earth could make a teenager smile if they didn't want to.

"Actually, they weren't all there."

"Oh?" If she had been a golden retriever, her ears would have just pricked up. "Who was missing?"

"Angus walked in just after I did. He'd been back to their room to get a cardigan for his wife. And Travis and his wife and kid weren't there at all."

"Yeah, I remember someone mentioned that they

should tell Travis what had happened. He's the other son?"

"Yeah. The Kleins have three kids: Travis, Angus, and Stephanie."

"So Travis is the eldest son?"

I took a sip of coffee and shrugged. "No. But he's the one who's been tapped to take over the company when his dad retires."

"So, apart from Travis and his family, the others were together in the restaurant when you went to tell them, right? Giving them all a lovely alibi."

I cast my mind back, mentally picturing the little gathering around the table. "Yep. Mr and Mrs Klein, Stephanie and Donal, and Angus's wife, Delphine, were all there. And then Angus walked in a few moments later."

"Was he gone long enough to push Krystal off her balcony?"

"I'm not sure. Maybe? He supposedly went straight to his room and back, but who knows? It's a small hotel, he might have had time. Apart from him, the only ones missing were Travis and his wife and son."

"How old is the son? Old enough for us to be concerned with?"

"First off," I said, rolling my eyes, "we are not *concerned with* anything. This is all Detective McGovern's problem. And secondly, he's just a kid. I don't know, maybe sixteen or seventeen."

"Old enough, then."

"Oh, come on. Now you're really reaching. What possible reason could a sixteen-year-old kid have to throw poor Krystal off a balcony? He's probably too busy on his phone to even notice that she's alive."

"Well, she's not anymore, is she? And *somebody* killed her. So I say we need to find out where all three of them were."

"You mean *Detective McGovern* needs to find out where they were," I corrected her.

"Of course," she said, her tone oozing innocence. "Did I say *we*? I meant Detective McGovern, of course."

"Priya," I said warningly.

She just laughed and hung up.

CHAPTER 7

Maisie wrenched open the door before the echoes of the doorbell had faded.

"Charlie's here!" she shrieked, her curly hair bouncing as she jumped up and down with excitement. "And Rufus, too!"

She dropped to her knees to throw her arms around Rufus's neck, and he stood there, patiently wagging, until she released him. I was pretty sure she was more excited to see him than she was to see me.

"Then don't leave them standing on the doorstep," Curtis's deep voice called from farther in the house.

"Hi, Maisie Moo." I smiled as I stepped inside. Curtis lived in a small weatherboard cottage only a few blocks away from my place. Well, everything was only a few blocks away from my place in Sunny Bay. It was a very small town. The cottage was old and painted the soft green of eucalyptus leaves, which made it feel as though it had just emerged from the state forest that loomed behind it. I followed Maisie through the tiny lounge room toward the even tinier kitchen, sniffing appreciatively. "Something smells good."

Curtis was wearing grey track pants and a dark blue T-shirt under an apron that said *kiss the cook*. "That's your dinner," he said while I obeyed the instructions on the apron, standing on tiptoe to reach his lips. As he pulled me in for a proper kiss, I lost my balance and landed against his strong chest. It was like hitting a brick wall, though admittedly one that smelled of a cologne that always reminded me of summertime and frangipanis.

"Careful," he said, moving the wooden spoon he'd been using to stir some red sauce before I ended up with it in my hair.

"What are we having?"

"Spaghetti," Maisie said, still bouncing. "And Daddy's special garlic bread."

I raised an eyebrow at Curtis. "Why is it special?"

"If I told you, I'd have to kill you. It's an old family recipe."

I rolled my eyes. Surely there were only so many things you could do with garlic, butter, and bread. "Fine, keep your secrets. I don't care as long as it's good."

"It is," Maisie promised.

I smiled at her dad. "Anything that somebody else cooks for me always tastes amazing."

"Would you like some wine?" he asked. "I've opened a cab sav."

"Sounds great."

I helped Maisie set the table while Curtis served the

meal. He'd made a salad to go along with the pasta, which I thought was quite impressive. My ex-fiancé had always complained about salad. He called it rabbit food and didn't see why any man should have to eat it.

That was only one of many reasons I was glad he was now my *ex*-fiancé.

Rufus, under the impression that he was a much smaller dog, tried to tuck himself under the table so he could hoover up anything that happened to fall. Even though I'd fed him before we came, he liked to pretend he hadn't eaten in months, employing his soulful brown eyes to devastating effect. Unfortunately for him, Curtis's long legs and one large golden retriever couldn't both fit in the space under the small circular table, so he had to content himself with sitting by Maisie's chair instead. That was probably a better option anyway, since Maisie was more likely to succumb to a good boy's charms than either Curtis or myself.

"Cheers." Curtis raised his glass of red, and I clinked mine against it.

"This is really good," I said as I tucked into the spaghetti.

"This is perfect," he said, smiling at me over the rim of his glass, and I knew he wasn't talking about the food. "Dinner with my two favourite girls. What more could a man want?"

"Daddy, don't be silly," Maisie said, frowning up at him. "Charlie's not a girl. She's old."

We both burst out laughing, and Maisie was caught between being pleased that she'd made us laugh and annoyed because she couldn't work out what we were laughing at.

"Well, she *is*," she said, frowning at her father. "*I'm* a girl. Charlie is a *lady*."

"That's very true," he said, stifling a smile. "And do you know what else she is?"

She stared up at him with her big brown eyes, prepared to be amazed. "What?"

"A detective. She just found a key piece of evidence for Detective McGovern."

"Oh, that." Maisie dismissed my sleuthing skills as old news. "I already knew that."

"Technically, it wasn't even me who found it," I said. "It was Rufus."

Maisie rewarded him with a pat on the head. "He's such a clever boy."

"Mmm." I glanced at Curtis. "Detective McGovern didn't seem all that grateful."

Curtis helped himself to another slice of garlic bread, which was, as advertised, especially good. "That man hands out smiles as if each one cost him ten bucks. I wouldn't take too much notice of him. His bark is worse than his bite."

Maisie's eyes widened. "He *bites* people?"

"Not very often."

"Only the bad guys, right? The perp—the perpera-traterors?" She seemed quite anxious on that point, so he gravely reassured her that Detective McGovern only bit *perpetrators* who truly deserved it.

My lips twitched, but I managed to hide my smile behind another mouthful of spaghetti.

When dinner was over, the washing up done, and Maisie was finally in bed—after more stalling tactics than Rufus whenever I tried to banish him to the backyard—Curtis and I settled on the couch to watch a movie. I tucked my feet up next to me and leaned into his side, snuggling my head into his neck.

His arm settled around my shoulders as he scrolled through the options. He searched in vain for five minutes before handing me the remote. "You pick."

I paused, searching his face. "Are you okay? You seem kind of distracted."

He ran a hand over his short brown hair. He'd let it grow a little longer since summer, so that he no longer looked as though he'd just joined the army. "I'm fine." He flashed me a smile. "Just indecisive. I think it's your turn to pick, anyway."

"You say that now, but you'll be complaining as soon as I choose some sappy romance."

He leaned closer to give me a kiss. "I'm all for sappy romance."

But he still seemed a little off. "It's the court hearing, isn't it? We don't have to watch anything if you'd rather just chat."

The hearing was only ten days away, and he'd been on edge for weeks.

"You don't want to hear my troubles. This is supposed to be a nice, relaxing evening."

I sat up and fixed him with a stern look. "Of course I want to hear your troubles. That's my job."

A smile tugged at the corner of his mouth. "I thought your job was showing up Detective McGovern."

I sighed. "No, that seems to happen without me even trying. I'm talking about my job as your girlfriend. It's in the manual, right there in the section on Care and Feeding of Your Bloke."

He snorted. "You make it sound like I'm some exotic pet."

"Oh, no," I said earnestly. "Blokes aren't exotic at all. They're extremely commonplace. Terribly ordinary."

"No wonder Maisie likes you," he mused. "Sometimes you're as nutty as she is."

I batted my eyelids at him. "Why, thank you, Officer."

At least I had him smiling again.

"So, what does it say in the Girlfriend Manual, then?"

"That a good girlfriend listens to her man's woes and makes appropriate soothing noises. If the woes are particularly bad, the application of kisses might even be called for."

"Well, if kisses are on the menu, far be it from me to stand in your way."

"Not so fast." I held up a hand as he leaned in to steal a kiss. "First, we have to be sure your woes are kiss-worthy. You haven't told me what's bothering you yet."

His gaze held mine for a long moment. Those eyes of his —the deep brown of melted chocolate—were one of my favourite things about him. They were framed by lashes so long and luscious they almost looked fake. The overall effect was so powerfully attractive that I had been known to stare at him so intently that I forgot what we were talking about.

"Sometimes you're as bossy as Maisie, too," he said.

That's right, I was trying to get him to open up to me. We'd made some progress in that department in the half-year we'd been going out. He was a truly charming man, but he had quite the tendency to bottle things up inside and pretend outwardly that everything was fine.

Like many things, I blamed Kelly for that. Being married to someone so manipulative had taught him to hide his emotions so they couldn't be weaponised against him.

"Curtis," I said, abandoning the humorous approach. "You can talk to me. Is the lawyer worried?"

"He said he's confident." Curtis shrugged. "But then, he would say that, wouldn't he? He's not going to tell the guy who's paying him that he's throwing his money away on a fool's cause."

"It's not a fool's cause. I think you have a very good case. Surely, the judge will see it's not in Maisie's best interest to rip her away from her school, her friends, family, and everyone and everything she's ever known. You're her father, and you're a very engaged dad. She'd miss you like crazy."

He sighed. "You don't know Kelly. She'll be laying it on thick, making herself the victim again. Poor little rich girl, got in with the wrong crowd, only started taking drugs because she was so stressed by the divorce, Your Honour."

"I doubt she'll bring up her drug-taking history at all,"

I said. "It hardly makes her look like a shining example of motherhood, does it?"

"She just has such a way of twisting things. She'll make a big deal about being all clean now and point at her rich new partner who can provide the best European schools for Maisie."

I rubbed his arm, trying to provide comfort. "There's nothing wrong with the school here. And Maisie adores her teacher."

He let his head fall back against the couch and stared glumly up at the ceiling. "Yes, but Sunny Bay Primary doesn't have its own theatre or gym or indoor swimming pool." His voice was thick with loathing. "And Kelly's the mother. Judges always favour keeping kids with their mums if they can. The last judge gave her shared custody, for crying out loud, even though she was a wreck."

He really was down. It must be awful to have the threat of losing your child hanging over your head like this.

"Sure, judges favour the mother if the mother is *here*. But dragging Maisie halfway across the world, away from you and her grandmothers and everyone she's ever known —how can that be fair on her? No one is *forcing* Kelly to move. If she was so desperate to be with Maisie, she could just stay here. I'm sure the judge will see that."

"I hope you're right," he said.

But he didn't sound hopeful at all. He sounded like a man about to meet his executioner.

CHAPTER 8

On Monday morning, I rang the Metropole and asked to speak to Mr Klein. I'd uploaded all the photos from the shoot on Friday to an online gallery but had run into a problem. I'd been dealing with Krystal. She was the one who had contacted me and arranged the photo shoot. The only email I had was hers. But it seemed a little cold to send the gallery link to that address. What would I say? *Hi, Krystal, I know you're dead, but here's the gallery ready for viewing?*

I'd only meant to ask Mr Klein for an alternate email address, but then it occurred to me that even seeing the photos of Krystal could be upsetting for some people, so perhaps he would rather I didn't include the group photo with her in it. When I asked him, he said he would prefer for me to bring him proofs of the photos so that he could look at them and approve them on the spot. I guess he wasn't really an email kind of guy. He was probably used to having Krystal handle that sort of thing for him.

So, on Monday afternoon, I was knocking on the door of room 452. It was at the very end of the corridor, and when Stephanie Klein opened it for me, I discovered it was actually a corner suite with windows on two walls, looking out over a beautiful vista of Sunny Bay, which had turned on a lovely winter's day for the viewing pleasure of the suite's occupants.

There was quite a crowd gathered. Not only Mr and Mrs Klein but Stephanie, Angus, and Angus's wife Delphine were lounging around a coffee table littered with the remnants of their afternoon tea.

Angus stood up as I walked in. "Well, I'll leave you to chat with Charlie," he said to his mum and dad. "Coming, Delphine?"

"We'll catch you at dinnertime," Delphine said, putting down her coffee cup and following him out the door.

"Sit down, Charlie." Mr Klein indicated the couch they'd just vacated. "Let's see these photos."

Rather than printing them out, I had brought my tablet with me, loaded up with the photos from the gallery. I handed it over, Stephanie squished herself onto the arm of her parents' couch so she could see, and the three Kleins swiped through, admiring the images.

"I wasn't sure if you'd still be here," I said, watching them. I'd been in business about nine months, so I was more used to people evaluating my work, but it still made me nervous. What if the client didn't like the photos I'd taken? So far, it hadn't been a problem, but there was always a first time. And this time, there could be an issue.

Would they want me to reshoot the group photo of the staff to remove the spectre of poor, dead Krystal reminding them of their loss? "I thought your conference would be over."

Mrs Klein sighed, but it was Stephanie who answered. "The police asked us to stay here while they completed their initial investigations."

"I can't believe someone could murder poor Krystal!" Mrs Klein burst out. Tears shone in her eyes. "She was such a lovely woman. What reason could anyone have to kill her?"

Stephanie patted her mother's shoulder. "Lovely women get killed all the time, Mum. The world is full of bad men."

Mr Klein set my tablet on the coffee table. Clearly, everyone was done with looking at photos. "You don't know that it was a man," he said. "The police haven't charged anyone yet."

"Oh, come on, Dad." Stephanie circled the couch and dropped into the armchair she'd been sitting in when I arrived. "We all know it was Justin."

"Stephanie!" Mrs Klein said.

"Who else would it be?" Her challenging stare shifted from her parents to me, as if she were daring me to argue. "They left together after dinner, and the rest of us were still there. Who else had an opportunity?"

I cleared my throat. "When I came to find you all in the restaurant, not everyone was there." I tried very hard not to sound as if I were accusing anyone of anything. Just stating a fact. I agreed with Stephanie—Justin certainly seemed the most likely suspect.

"Well, yeah. Travis and the others had gone." She waved a hand, as if this had no bearing on the case. "But they'd gone back to their rooms."

That wasn't any kind of alibi. "Angus wasn't there, either."

"He was only gone a few minutes," she said dismissively.

"Can't a man take a leak in peace without being suspected of something?" Mr Klein added with a belligerent set to his square jaw.

"He didn't go to the bathroom, Dad," Stephanie reminded him. "He went to get a cardigan for Delphine, remember?"

"He's always running after that woman," he grumbled. "Can't even dress herself for the weather."

Mrs Klein laid a conciliatory hand on his arm. "It *was* quite cold in that restaurant, dear. And the vent was right above poor Delphine."

"When did Krystal and Justin leave the restaurant?" I asked.

Stephanie looked at her parents. "I don't know. Maybe around eight thirty? I wasn't really paying attention to the time."

"Was there some reason they left? Were you all finished dinner by then?"

"Dinner was over, but most of us were still chatting over coffee."

"We were talking about family things," Mrs Klein said.

"Reminiscing about when the kids were small. It probably wasn't very interesting for Krystal and Justin, so they excused themselves."

"And then they went to the bar?"

"Did they?" She blinked at me like an owl caught out in the daylight. I wondered whether someone had given her a sedative to cope with the trauma. "They didn't say where they were going. They said goodnight and I assumed they were going back to their room."

Mr Klein sat forward eagerly. "Are you taking on the case? I hoped you would."

Taking on the case? "I'm not an investigator, Mr Klein. I'm a photographer."

"Yes, yes." He waved away my photography skills. "But you've done this before, haven't you? Solved a case when the police couldn't?"

"Just a matter of being in the right place at the right time," I said.

"And here you are again," he said. "Right place, right time. And asking all the right questions, too. Go on, go on."

A little thrown, I took a minute to gather my thoughts. But if he was happy to answer, why not ask? It couldn't do any harm to get a clearer picture of what had happened. "When did Travis and his family leave?"

"Not that long before you came in." Stephanie said, sounding unsure. "Maybe ten minutes?"

"So about nine, or five past." Krystal had fallen at five minutes past nine, so any one of them could have pushed her, if that timing was correct.

Mr Klein nodded. "That sounds about right. Travis said he had to call a client before it got too late."

"And Yumi had a headache," Mrs Klein added. "The poor girl suffers a lot with migraines."

"Well, Brandon left before that," Stephanie said. "Travis's son. About the same time Krystal and Justin did, actually. But Travis and Yumi were only a few minutes ahead of you."

Phrases like *a few minutes* were useless in circumstances like these. The difference between five minutes and fifteen was the difference between a watertight alibi and a possible murderer. Krystal fell at 9:05; I'd gone upstairs to the restaurant about 9:15. If Travis and his wife had left at nine, they were suspects, but if it had been ten past, they were in the clear.

I sighed. "I don't suppose you can be more precise about when Travis left? Or Angus?"

Stephanie shrugged. "No, sorry."

And what about Brandon? I had a hard time imagining he could be the killer, but if he'd left when Krystal and Justin did, he certainly had the opportunity. "Why did Brandon leave so early?"

Stephanie snorted. "As if Brandon would hang around for a family conversation. That kid never talks to anyone. He's always on his phone."

"He's shy," his grandmother said.

"He's *rude*," Stephanie countered.

Mr Klein scowled. "He's spoiled. He wanted to watch some live screen, so they said he could go back to his room."

"Livestream, Dad," Stephanie said.

He snorted impatiently. "I don't care what it's called. In my day, we all managed just fine without being glued to our phones every waking minute. They call them smartphones, but they're making everyone stupid. That boy can't even sit through an hour of dinner without feeling deprived. They should put him in the army—then he'd know what it's like to be deprived!"

"I'm sure Charlie doesn't want to hear our family issues," Mrs Klein said with a bright smile. "And Brandon's manners are irrelevant, since he clearly didn't push Krystal off her balcony."

I smiled back, though it wasn't as clear to me as to his grandmother. Still, it did seem unlikely. He was only sixteen or seventeen.

"True, true." Her husband nodded approvingly. "I can't help wondering if the police are barking up the wrong tree entirely. My guess is she surprised someone in the middle of a break-in, and the burglar attacked her."

"Or perhaps Justin decided pushing his wife off a balcony was easier than filing for divorce," Stephanie said. "I don't think they were very happy together."

"Nonsense," Mr Klein said in a bracing tone. "We're a family values company. None of my people would ever do such a thing."

"Yeah, but he wasn't one of your people, was he? Just married to one of them."

This was like watching a tennis match. Or a joust. Stephanie seemed determined to pin this on Justin.

Her father levelled a stern glare at her. "We shouldn't

be hurling unfounded accusations around. There's no need to drag the company name through the mud when all we have are suspicions. I still firmly believe an outside party was responsible." He turned to me. "Wouldn't you agree, Charlie?"

"I suppose it's possible," I said cautiously.

"I'm sure the police only suspect Justin of murder because of that shoe being found," Mr Klein said, his voice full of frustration. I cringed inwardly, but he didn't seem to be blaming me; in all likelihood, the police hadn't told him who had found the shoe. "But I'm sure there must be some sensible explanation."

Stephanie rolled her eyes so hard I was surprised they didn't plop onto the plush blue carpet and keep rolling right under the coffee table. "You bet there's a sensible explanation. The only one that makes sense is, in fact, that Justin killed Krystal."

Mr Klein turned to me in appeal. "Charlie, you're familiar with these local boys. Can you tell me, hand on heart, that that McGovern fella will look for another explanation if he thinks he's already found his man in Justin?"

There was a short silence. All three pairs of eyes rested on me as I floundered for something to say. Mr Klein took my silence as agreement.

"Just as I thought. Justin needs someone in his corner. I asked you here today, Charlie, partly to look at these lovely photos"—he gestured at the now-black screen of the tablet—"and partly because I thought, with your experience, you might be that person."

I shifted uncomfortably. "Surely, Justin needs a lawyer in his corner. I'm not sure what use I could possibly be."

"But you saved the day with that robbery investigation at Christmastime, didn't you? They would never have found that necklace if it wasn't for you."

"That was a fluke," I said hurriedly. "Just a lucky guess. I certainly can't interfere in a police investigation." Well, not again, anyway. Goodness knows I'd already done it far too many times. At this rate, Detective McGovern would be looking for a voodoo doll of me to stick pins in.

"Not even if we paid you?" Mr Klein clearly didn't want to let go of the idea. "Klein's World of Kristmas may have fallen on hard times, but we're not so badly off that we can't support our own people. We would make it worth your while."

"Really, Mr Klein, it would be highly inappropriate."

Mr Klein sighed heavily but didn't try to persuade me any further. We seemed to be at an impasse. Mrs Klein finally broke the silence.

"You know, dear," she said to her husband, "perhaps poor Krystal did have enemies. She was a lovely girl, but she could be quite cutting sometimes."

"Heavens, yes." Stephanie sat back and crossed her legs as if she was settling in for a long and juicy conversation. "She was always saying the most outrageously insulting things to people and then pretending it was a joke if they took offence."

"People are too easily offended these days," her father muttered. "It's not Krystal's fault if people don't have a sense of humour."

I gathered from that that Krystal's boss had never been the butt of her jokes.

"You thought it was funny how she mocked Delphine's accent all the time?" Stephanie asked. "Or how she used to announce to the office every time Donal hurt himself, so that we could all laugh at how accident-prone he is?"

"Is he?" I couldn't help asking. "Accident-prone, I mean?"

Mrs Klein smiled indulgently. "Oh, yes. He was always like that, even as a boy. My sister Pam used to complain she could never get a photo of him where he didn't have skinned knees or an arm in a sling or some kind of scrape on his face."

"He's a magnet for paper cuts," Stephanie agreed. "I wouldn't have been surprised in the slightest if someone told me *Donal* fell off a balcony. It would be so like him. Krystal's comments never seemed to bother him, but it was just so unnecessary. It was like Krystal was stuck back in high school being the popular kid, laughing at all the nerdy ones."

"You just didn't appreciate her sense of humour," Mr Klein said. "Donal needs to man up if he can't take a few jokes."

His daughter gave him an exasperated look. "*Nobody* liked being the butt of her so-called jokes. Ask Angus how funny he found it every time she explained something really basic to him, pretending that she thought he wouldn't be able to understand it. She used to go on and on with her snide comments about the benefits of a good

73

education." Stephanie turned to me. "Angus was the only one of us who didn't go to university. He can be a little touchy about it. Krystal had a knack for ferreting out people's weaknesses."

There was a knock at the door, and Stephanie stood to open it, revealing Donal himself standing there.

"I was just walking down to the surf club to grab a coffee," he said. "Does anyone else want one? Steph? Auntie Susan?"

"No, thank you, dear." Mrs Klein smiled at him. She indicated the remains of their afternoon tea. "We've just had something."

"What on earth have you done to your face?" Stephanie asked. She was still holding the door open while Donal lurked awkwardly just inside the room. A small purple bruise had bloomed on his chin since I'd seen him on Friday night.

He rubbed his jaw ruefully. "I got up to go to the bathroom in the middle of the night and didn't turn on the light. Walked straight into the door frame."

Behind his back, Stephanie rolled her eyes and grinned at me as if to say, *See? I told you he was a walking disaster zone.*

He left as soon as he was sure no one needed anything, and I stood up to go, too. "I'll leave you one of my cards." I picked up my tablet and left a card in its place. *Charlie Carter Photography*. I was still inordinately proud of my growing little business and all the skills it was teaching me. This wasn't where I thought I'd end up, but I was very happy with how my life was turning out. "Let me know which ones you want printed, if any."

"Thank you for coming," Mrs Klein said. "The photos are lovely."

"Yes, thank you, Charlie," Mr Klein echoed. "Are you sure I can't persuade you to help Justin out with this investigation?"

"Daaad," Stephanie said, rolling her eyes again. She opened the door for me, and I paused. Stephanie's opinion of Krystal seemed a lot different to her father's.

"Did Krystal seem changed recently?" I asked her in a low tone. "More anxious or secretive?"

"Not at all. I bet she never even saw it coming." Stephanie's mouth quirked in a rueful line as she met my eyes. "You'll have guessed I wasn't a big Krystal fan, but still, it's pretty brutal to have your life snatched away from you like that. I hope they find whoever did it, Justin or not."

"Let's hope so," I said.

CHAPTER 9

I was in a thoughtful mood as I headed back down the corridor toward the lifts. For a family company, there seemed to be some tensions among the staff of Klein's World of Kristmas. Krystal making digs at Angus about his lack of tertiary education, Stephanie's clear dislike of her, and Mr Klein standing up for her bullying behaviour. And it seemed, from the little touches on his arm and the way she spoke to him, that Mrs Klein was used to handling her husband's outbursts.

I'd dealt with men like him in my former life working in HR. A little bit of success went to the head of a certain type of man, who then began to believe that he was far better at his job than he actually was. Such men attributed their success to their own magnificence rather than a combination of luck, connections, and just being in the right place at the right time. Their heads swelled along with their demands, and before you knew it, you had a little dictator in the making, someone who was convinced that their every decision was the correct one and no one else's opinion mattered. It took a great deal of finesse to manage a man like that, and I imagined that Mrs Klein had had many years of practice.

Krystal also must have been good at soothing his temper and gratifying his ego, considering how highly he spoke of her. I wondered what Stephanie had seen that her father hadn't, and whether the problem was really with Krystal or with Stephanie herself. People were so complicated—they could come to dislike someone for any reason, no matter how irrelevant or irrational.

Perhaps Mr Klein was perfectly justified in defending his personal assistant. Stephanie might be the one who had Krystal all wrong. It was hard to tell, having exchanged no more than a few words with the dead woman myself. She'd seemed pleasant, highly efficient, and good at her job, but that meant very little. Priya often accused me of being too gullible, of taking everyone at face value and assuming they were good people. But it was less me being gullible and more that I liked to give people the benefit of the doubt.

As I turned a corner to the last stretch of corridor before the lifts, I noticed a door ahead of me swinging closed. This wouldn't normally have been any cause for concern, since guests and staff went in and out of doors plenty in the course of their days. The problem was that *this* door still had blue- and white-checked police tape tacked over it.

Krystal's room. And the figure who'd entered wasn't wearing a police uniform.

Or anything that suggested they belonged to the forensics team or the coroner's office, for that matter. I'd only seen him from the back, but the dark-haired man had been wearing casual pants and a white T-shirt, and there'd been something about him that rang a bell. Though I couldn't immediately pinpoint who it was, my subconscious was telling me it was someone I knew. Someone who should *not* be entering room 428.

Before I'd even thought about my next move, my body took over. I hurried down the corridor and grabbed the door before it shut. Then my brain caught up. Did I really want to get involved? I was going to look pretty stupid if it was just some hotel worker with a perfectly valid reason for entering the room.

But, surely, even a hotel worker would have to respect the police tape. I listened, but I didn't hear anyone moving around inside. Cautiously, I pushed the door open wider.

It was a typical hotel room layout. A narrow section faced me, making room for a bathroom on the left, whose door was currently closed. Past the bathroom was a wardrobe with a sliding mirror door, which was open enough to show a white towelling robe and a couple of dresses hanging from the rack. Beyond that, the room opened out. From my vantage point at the door, I could see part of a neatly made bed, a desk and chair, a large TV on the wall, and a small lounge upholstered in a blue that matched the curtains. They were currently open, allowing a view of the balcony outside. No sign of the man I had followed.

I heard someone moving around behind the closed

bathroom door. Surely, someone hadn't sneaked in here just to use the bathroom. And how had they gotten in if the door was locked?

I took another step into the room, my hand still on the door. A peculiar hollow clunk sounded from inside the bathroom. A moment later, the bathroom door opened. Travis Klein started at the sight of me standing there, close enough to touch.

"You scared me," he said, withdrawing a hand from the pocket of his pants. What had he just put in there? Was he stealing the complementary soaps? There was a bulge that might have been a mobile phone or perhaps a wallet.

"What were you doing in there?" I asked. "This is a crime scene. You shouldn't be in here at all."

He closed the bathroom door behind him and stepped into the narrow space beside the half-open wardrobe, crowding me back into the doorway of the room. He turned a sorrowful look on me. "I know it's wrong, but I needed to see the place where she died. I suppose I was just looking for some kind of closure. This whole thing doesn't seem real."

"She didn't die in the bathroom," I said sharply.

"No, of course not." He shot me a megawatt smile. It was the kind of smile you see on TV evangelists, or actors spruiking their latest movie. The kind that said, *Oh, don't mind me, I'm just a down-home guy being all charming*. "I thought I might be able to smell her perfume in there. She wore a very distinctive scent, you know."

"Really?" I didn't remember Krystal having any particular scent, but I had only met her the once, so I supposed it might be true. I wondered what his wife would think of him wandering around sniffing for a dead woman's perfume. My gaze dropped momentarily to his trouser pocket again. Had he stolen a bottle of Krystal's perfume from her bathroom? How bizarre that would be.

"How did you get in?"

"It was open." He gestured toward the open doorway and the corridor behind me. "Shall we?"

It was open, my left butt cheek. As if the police would have left their crime scene unsecured. Detective McGovern would have a coronary at the very suggestion. I might not like the guy very much, but I had more respect for him than that.

Besides, modern hotel room doors locked automatically when they closed. That was why I'd hurried to stop it closing when I first saw Travis entering the room. Was he seriously expecting me to believe that McGovern had intentionally arranged to keep the door of his crime scene open?

When I didn't move, Travis said, "You're right, we should leave. There's nothing to see in here anyway." He heaved a deep sigh. "Poor Krystal. I still can't believe it."

Well, that made two of us who were having problems with belief. Priya would be so proud of me. I might like to think the best of people, but Travis Klein was giving me real problems in that department. In fact, I'd go so far as to assume he must have gotten whatever he came for, considering how keen he was to leave all of a sudden.

I stepped back, ducking under the police tape, and he

followed me into the hallway. The door slammed shut behind us. I jiggled the handle, just to be sure.

Of course, it was locked, just as I'd expected. The only way to get back in now was to use a keycard. The Metropole might have stood on the headland overlooking Sunny Bay for almost a century, but the interiors had had quite a few facelifts in that time. Room security had been upgraded to a computerised system that matched every other modern hotel I'd seen.

I braced myself for a plea not to mention Travis's little trespass to anyone, but he didn't go there.

"How did the photos turn out?" he asked as we walked the short distance to the lifts.

"Good. I've just come from showing them to your mum and dad, actually."

"And what did they think?" He turned that professional smile on me again, only slightly less blinding than before. He had very white, very even teeth, and I wondered if Mummy and Daddy had paid for them, and how much they'd cost. "I'm sure they were happy."

I nodded as he pressed the button to call the lift. "It's always good to have another satisfied customer."

"I bet you have a lot of those." The lift doors slid open soundlessly, and we stepped in. He cocked an eyebrow at me. "Which floor?"

"Ground for me."

He pressed the buttons for level three and the ground floor. The lift doors closed, reflecting our faces back at us in their mirrored surfaces. A faint whiff of perfume hung on the still air—the ghost of someone's aftershave, perhaps.

"Have a nice day," Travis said when the doors opened on his floor a few seconds later.

"You, too," I said automatically, though, in fact, I rather hoped he *didn't* have a good day. The kind of person who went poking around in crime scenes didn't deserve one.

On impulse, I hit the button to keep the doors open and watched him stride down the hallway. He said hello to a maid standing by her housekeeping trolley farther down the hall, but he didn't go more than a few doors down. He stopped beside a particularly ugly painting and pulled out his keycard, letting himself into his room. Only then did I release the button and let the lift doors close.

There was something very suspicious about Mr Travis Klein.

CHAPTER 10

Tuesday night was our monthly book club meeting, so we met at the library, surrounded by the distinctive scent of old books and lulled by the soft hum of the air-conditioning. We usually gathered in the children's section of the library, where there were beanbags and armchairs and a relaxed atmosphere. I liked the bright colours, and Andrea often had some kind of fun display on the walls. This month, there was a jungle theme, and a gigantic crêpe paper giraffe gazed down on us benignly as we chatted.

I had given up on *Madame Bovary* partway through, but I was hoping to hide it by making vague statements and nodding along with others' opinions.

"What did you think of the book, Charlie?" Andrea asked as soon as we were settled in our circle.

Of course she'd started with me. Good thing I had also used Priya's trick and looked up a summary of the story online. "I can't say I was a fan. She has an unhappy marriage, she has affairs. Everyone is miserable, she dies, the end."

We were a small group tonight. Emily and Sarah were both busy, and Jack, our token male, had a shift at the hospital. I'd noticed Priya's look of disappointment when I walked in without him.

Andrea laughed. "There were interesting themes of desire and obsession," she said. "And what about its exploration of the gap between fantasy and reality? That was sublime."

I shrugged. "The fantasies of bored housewives don't really do it for me. I'd much prefer an actual fantasy. Give me a dragon any day." Any kind of fantasy was preferable to a well-written but miserable literary masterpiece, as far as I was concerned.

"I have to say I'm with Charlie on this one." Heidi gave me a conspiratorial grin. "I find the older I get, the more I look for a happy ending. There's too much misery in the world to be reading about it in books as well."

"That's right," I said, happy to have found an ally. "Books are my happy place."

"Books are art and meaning," Andrea said.

"Books are whatever we need them to be," Aunt Evie said, joining the fray from the bright green armchair on my left. "They're magic, they're entertainment. They are our confidantes and our therapists, our ways of making sense of the world."

Andrea's eyes lit up with enthusiasm. "I couldn't agree more."

I smiled at my aunt. "That's very deep for you. Are you feeling okay?"

She smacked me lightly on the arm. "So cheeky!"

I didn't contribute a great deal to the discussion after that. I really hadn't enjoyed the parts of the book I'd read and found it difficult to see all the marvellous qualities in it that Andrea did. Heidi didn't have a lot to say, either, though that changed once the literary portion of the evening had concluded and we all moved into the small librarians' kitchen to make cups of tea and eat the cake Aunt Evie had brought.

"Cake, Priya? What about you, Heidi?" Aunt Evie offered generous slices to everyone. "It's the lemon one you like."

An expression almost of revulsion flitted across Heidi's face. "Not for me, thanks. I heard the police are talking to that poor woman's husband again."

None of us needed to ask who she meant by *that poor woman*.

"He doesn't look like a killer to me," Aunt Evie mused.

"You went out with a killer once," Priya reminded her, "so I don't think we should take your impressions into consideration."

Aunt Evie rolled her eyes. "Make one mistake around here and they hold it against you forever."

"And Justin certainly seemed to have anger management issues," Priya added.

I nodded, remembering that intense, serious conversation we had all witnessed between him and Krystal at the bar. How he had grabbed at her arm, forcing her to stay when she had first tried to leave, and how she'd stormed off with him striding purposefully after her. To kill her? I shivered.

"I saw him outside the ice cream shop that night," Heidi said.

"When?" Priya asked, looking confused. "Before we met for drinks?"

"No, after. I was on the way home, and I suddenly got a craving for liquorice ice cream."

"Ugh." Andrea pulled a revolted face. "Liquorice ice cream? What is *wrong* with you?"

Heidi laughed. "I know it's not for everyone, but the one they make at the ice cream shop in town is really good."

"I'll take your word for that," Andrea said with a shudder.

"Anyway, I got a parking spot outside the fish and chip place, and as I was walking up to the ice cream shop, I saw Justin outside the tattoo parlour across the street, talking to some kid. They seemed to know each other."

Aunt Evie frowned. "They don't have children, do they?"

I shook my head.

"He was too old to be Justin's," Heidi said. "And anyway he was Asian."

I immediately thought of Travis's surly son. "How old was this kid?"

She shrugged. "I don't know. A teenager ... fifteen or sixteen, I suppose."

"It can't have been Justin," Priya said, refusing to be distracted by teenagers.

"It was," Heidi insisted. "He was wearing that same dreadful shirt we saw in the bar."

"The one with the flamingos?" Aunt Evie asked. "I rather liked it. It was cheerful."

"Leaving aside your questionable fashion sense," Priya said, "if it was Justin, he couldn't have been the one to kill Krystal. The timing's too tight. Unless you drove really slowly to the ice cream shop?" she added with a hopeful look at Heidi.

"I drove at a normal speed," Heidi said. "How long after I left did Krystal die?"

We all looked at each other. "It was only about five minutes, I think," I said.

"And you didn't stay chatting to Andrea in the carpark?" Priya seemed very reluctant to lose Justin as her prime suspect.

"No, we both went straight to our cars," Andrea said.

"So he would have had only seconds to get to the ice cream place after throwing her off the balcony," Aunt Evie said, looking thoughtful. "It couldn't be done."

I was doing the same maths in my head. A minute for Heidi to walk to her car after she said goodnight to us, a couple more minutes to drive down the hill into town, a minute to find a parking spot, then another to walk up the street to the ice cream shop—and Justin had already been there. If he was already chatting to Travis's son outside the tattoo parlour at the time of her death, it simply wasn't possible that he could have killed Krystal. And neither could the kid.

"Not unless he had a teleporter," Heidi agreed.

"But then why would he say he was walking on the beach alone if he had a perfectly good alibi, with Travis's son to back him up?" I pulled out my phone and quickly brought up the group photo of the assembled Klein clan, with Brandon glowering at the camera on the end of the line. "Is this the kid you saw?"

Heidi leaned over to inspect the photo. "Could be. I mean, I only glanced at them, and I was mainly looking at Justin, wondering if he'd calmed down after that scene in the bar. But like I said, they seemed to know each other, so it probably was him."

"And *had* Justin calmed down?" Aunt Evie asked.

She shrugged. "He seemed fine, but he didn't stay long. By the time I got my ice cream and came out, he was gone. The kid was still there, though." She contemplated the photo with a frown. "He was with another boy, then, who had his beanie pulled so far down it was a wonder he could see where he was going."

"Never mind the kid," Priya said impatiently. "Charlie's right—it doesn't make sense for Justin to lie about his whereabouts if he had a perfectly good alibi."

"Unless he was doing something wrong," Aunt Evie said.

"What, worse than murdering his wife?" Andrea scoffed.

"There's no law against standing outside tattoo parlours chatting," I said. Though it was odd.

"Maybe he was casing the joint," Aunt Evie suggested.

"Anyway, you need to talk to the police," Priya said to Heidi. "Tell them that you saw Justin."

"Yes, I suppose I should. I didn't realise it was so important."

Priya sat back and folded her arms, a disgruntled expression on her face. "But if Justin didn't do it, who did?"

"That's the million-dollar question," Aunt Evie said. "Who indeed?"

"Why are you all looking at me?" I asked in the sudden silence.

Aunt Evie looked hopeful. "You must have *some* ideas."

"Well ..." I had vowed not to get involved this time. To leave Detective McGovern to his job without interference. He had certainly managed to solve crimes without my help before I'd moved to Sunny Bay, and he would no doubt manage just fine on his own this time, too.

But somehow, I already seemed to be involved. I wasn't sure how that kept happening, but there was no denying that I did have some ideas, and I felt compelled to share them. The thought that the killer might get away with poor Krystal's death didn't sit right with me.

Aunt Evie leaned forward eagerly in her seat. "Who do you think it is?"

"The old guy?" Priya asked. "She was his secretary. I bet they were having an affair."

"Really?" Aunt Evie looked a little scandalised. "He's a *lot* older than her."

"When has that ever stopped anyone?" Andrea said.

"Maybe she was demanding he leave his wife, so he decided to kill her."

They all looked at me for confirmation. Even though it was a serious subject, I had to laugh. "I think you guys are getting carried away. I don't think Mr Klein's the type. He's always talking about his family values."

"Well, of course he would *say* that," Andrea said darkly. "Talk is cheap."

Heidi shook her head. "You're such a cynic, Andrea."

Andrea's generally negative opinion of the opposite sex had softened since she'd started going out with Nick, a lovely guy she'd met at her gym, but the scars of her failed marriage still showed sometimes. "Am I? Or am I a realist?"

"Well, anyway, I don't think Mr Klein had anything to do with it," I went on. "I'm actually wondering about one of his sons. I caught Travis going into the crime scene yesterday."

That got their attention.

Priya's eyes widened. "What?"

"Why?" Heidi asked.

"Good question. He said he missed her and he wanted to smell her perfume—"

"A likely story," Aunt Evie scoffed.

"Yeah, I didn't believe him, either. But I don't know what he was actually doing." I told them everything that had happened, including hearing that odd bang from the bathroom, and how keen Travis had seemed to leave, as if he'd gotten what he came for.

"That sounds very suspicious," Heidi said. "Did you tell Detective McGovern?"

"I rang him yesterday and left a message. I said I had some information for him to do with the case, but he hasn't called me back yet."

"I'm sure he's very busy with the investigation," Aunt Evie said.

"Either that or he hates you," Priya suggested with a smirk.

I sighed. "He'll hate me even more when I tell him that I entered his crime scene."

Aunt Evie patted my hand reassuringly. "But only in pursuit of a suspect, dear. I'm sure that's allowed."

Maybe it was allowed for officers. I wasn't so sure Detective McGovern would be understanding. I could easily imagine what he'd say, and it would contain words like "contaminating a crime scene" and "interfering civilians".

"It serves him right for leaving it unlocked," Heidi said with fierce loyalty. "If he didn't want people wandering in, he should have made sure it was properly secure."

"That's the thing, though," I said. That point had been troubling me. "Those hotel doors lock automatically when they close. I checked when we left the room, and it was locked."

"So how did Travis get in?" Aunt Evie asked.

That was an excellent question—one that Detective McGovern would have to find the answer to.

If he ever called me back.

CHAPTER 11

THE NEXT MORNING, DETECTIVE MCGOVERN STILL HADN'T returned my call, and I was starting to feel almost as bad as if I were the one who'd committed the crime. Travis had entered room 428 on Monday afternoon. It was now nearly lunchtime on Wednesday—almost forty-eight hours later, and the police still didn't know about it. This was vital information, and I could only imagine how impressed the grumpy detective would be that I'd kept it to myself for so long.

"Of course, it would help if he ever returned his phone calls," I told Rufus as I pegged the last of a load of washing on the line. It was a beautiful winter's day, and the washing would be dry in no time.

Rufus was currently sprawled on his back in the grass nearby, soaking up the sun, letting a gentle breeze ruffle the long hairs on his belly and chest. One ear twitched at the sound of my voice, but he didn't bother opening his eyes.

I crouched down and rubbed his soft belly. "I should call him again, shouldn't I?"

Rufus had no opinion on the matter, but I pulled my phone out of my back pocket and dialled the detective's number. The same old voicemail directed me to leave a message, promising that McGovern would get back to me "at his earliest convenience".

"Ha." I hung up, frowning. "He says that, but it's all lies. I swear he has no intention of ever calling me back. Well, if the mountain won't come to Mohammad ... maybe we should go for a walk. What do you think, boy?"

At the word *walk*, it was as if someone had zapped Rufus with a cattle prod. He flung himself violently to his feet in a scramble of limbs and fur, then stood, ears pricked and tail wagging furiously.

I rubbed his head as I stood up. "I guess that's a yes."

It was a while since we'd had a decent walk. The weather had been cold and windy, so we'd kept our excursions short. The police station was in the next town over, Waterloo Bay. It was a brisk forty-minute walk from my place along the foreshore, then inland along a very nice bike trail through the coastal scrub before hitting the town's outer streets. Rufus had a marvellous time sniffing all the new smells along the trail and barking at seagulls and cockatoos. He had a deep and abiding hatred of cockatoos, which mainly amounted to barking ferociously at them if they dared to strut around on the grass looking for seeds anywhere in his vicinity. Occasionally, he would lunge at one, but he'd been a bit half-hearted about that since the memorable day he'd actually caught one and had absolutely no idea what to do with the squawking, flapping thing.

The weather continued to be beautiful. By the time we arrived at the police station, I was quite warm and Rufus's tongue was hanging out of his mouth. It was a pale brick building behind the main shopping area, with tinted glass doors and an odd lack of windows. Sturdy gum trees shaded the carpark at the side. Curtis was always complaining about the birds that sat in those trees and dropped little bombs all over his nice, clean police cruiser.

Much to Rufus's chagrin, I clipped his lead on and tied him to the pole of a street sign out front. Normally, I let him roam, but the lead was useful for situations like this, where a dog wouldn't be welcome inside.

"Don't look at me like that." I dug his collapsible bowl out of my backpack and poured some water into it from my drink bottle. "I won't be gone long, and Detective McGovern is already annoyed with you for getting your spit all over that shoe you found."

Rufus slurped some water from the bowl, scattering drops on the pavement and my shoes. He approached drinking with the same enthusiasm he did everything else, so it was always a messy affair. Meanwhile, I took a long drink myself. Even in winter, walking was thirsty work. Then I packed the bottle away with a sigh. I couldn't put this off any longer.

"Wish me luck."

Rufus wagged his tail lazily and flopped down on the pavement, panting. I straightened my shoulders and took the front steps two at a time.

Inside, the foyer was empty, although behind the glass screens the office was in disarray, with filing boxes and pile of paper heaped on every flat surface. The officer on duty looked up as I entered and smiled. He was an older man whose belly threatened to pop the buttons on his uniform shirt. His greying beard and blue eyes made me think of Santa Claus. "Can I help you?"

I looked past him into the large, busy room behind him. The desk where Detective McGovern had been working last time was empty.

"Hi." I smiled, nervous butterflies fluttering in my stomach now I was here. "I was hoping to have a quick word with Detective McGovern."

"What's your name?"

"Charlie Carter."

He picked up the phone and dialled. "Charlie Carter to see you, Luke."

Funny. I'd known McGovern's name was Luke—I'd seen it on his business cards—but I'd never actually heard anyone call him that before. It made him sound more like a real human being.

The officer hung up. "He'll be out in a minute. Take a seat."

He gestured at the hard plastic chairs lined up against the glass of the entrance wall. I spotted Rufus outside, still panting. I stepped back from the counter but was too edgy to sit. *Don't be ridiculous*, I told myself firmly. *You're not a naughty kid waiting to see the principal. You haven't done anything wrong.*

But my stomach still dropped into my boots when

Detective McGovern emerged from a corridor, striding through the cluttered desks toward me. He was wearing a blue and grey vest that looked hand-knitted over his white shirt, and it occurred to me that I knew nothing about the man. Who in his life was knitting him vests? Was he married? Heaven forbid. Or did he have some sweet old grandma knitting for her little Lukey?

Neither option seemed possible. He was just Detective McGovern, perpetually frowning, always annoyed with me.

"Miss Carter." He didn't smile, but at least he wasn't frowning. Yet. "What can I do for you?"

I smiled nervously. "I saw something that I think you should know about. Pertaining to the murder of Krystal Dendekker."

Pertaining to the murder. Good heavens. I sounded like a character in an Agatha Christie novel. That was what nerves did to me.

Aaand there was the frown. "You'd better come in." He opened the door and led the way back through the busy open plan office full of people on phones and officers moving briskly between the desks. I looked around for Curtis, but he wasn't there. I knew he was working today but he was probably out on patrol.

I'd been back here before, to the little interview rooms, but we didn't go there today. Detective McGovern took the seat behind a relatively tidy desk tucked into a corner of the large room and motioned for me to take the visitor's chair opposite. Once I was settled, he folded his hands on top of the desk and raised a brow. "Well, Miss Carter? What's this about?"

I could tell from the hard set of his mouth that he was feeling impatient. Probably thinking that I'd come here on some flimsy excuse to try to insert myself into his case or to wheedle information from him that I shouldn't, when, in fact, all I was doing was my civic duty.

I sat up straighter, determined not to be cowed by the disgruntled detective. "It's about Travis Klein." I drew in a deep, fortifying breath, then came out with it in a rush. "I saw him entering the crime scene on Monday afternoon."

McGovern's eyebrows drew together. "Entering the *crime scene*?"

I nodded. "I'd been to see the Kleins in their suite, and I was heading back toward the lift. As I came around the corner of the corridor, I saw Travis Klein's back as he went inside room 428."

He dragged a notepad across the desk toward him. "What time was this?"

"About two-thirty, I think."

He noted it down and spoke again without looking at me. "Did he see you?"

I paused. This was the awkward part. "Well, not then."

He looked up, suspicion in his eyes. "Go on."

"I thought someone should see what he was doing in there, so I followed him."

"Into the crime scene."

"Yes."

"The crime scene that was cordoned off with police tape."

I squirmed in my seat. "Yes. But I only stood in the doorway. He was in the bathroom with the door shut. I heard him moving around, and there was an odd banging sound, then he came out and found me there."

He put his pen down and sat back in his seat. "Miss Carter, do you realise how serious this is? You could have jeopardised this whole investigation because you thought *someone should see what he was doing in there*." He mimicked me in a very unpleasant way. "You keep saying you want to help, but do you realise what you've done could get the whole case thrown out of court? All the defence has to do is tell the jury that random people were tramping through the crime scene and maybe *they* were the ones who left that crucial piece of evidence behind, and the defendant gets off scot-free."

"I didn't touch anything," I said hastily.

"This isn't the first time you've interfered in my investigations," he continued as if I hadn't spoken. A muscle jumped in his jaw. "Do you *want* me to arrest you? Because I will if you don't stop playing amateur detective."

"I wasn't playing amateur detective." This was going just as badly as I had feared. "I was just walking past and I saw Travis. *He* was the one who was interfering with the crime scene."

"And I suppose if Travis jumped off a cliff, you would, too?"

Wow. That was a low blow. "Don't you want to know what he was doing in there?"

He folded his arms and scowled at me. "Amaze me. I'm sure you've solved the whole case."

"Well, I think he went in to get something, because of all that noise in the bathroom, and he seemed very keen to leave as soon as he came out."

"You *think*. What did he actually say he was doing?"

"That he wanted to smell Krystal's perfume."

Detective McGovern rolled his eyes. At least we agreed on something. "And how did he get in?"

"He said it was open."

McGovern sat up abruptly. "That's a load of rubbish. Those doors lock as soon as they close. Do you think I'm so incompetent that I wouldn't make sure the door of the crime scene was *closed*?"

"No, of course not." *Ugh, McGovern.* To think I'd been defending this guy to all my friends. "But he *did* get in."

"How?"

"I don't know. You could check with the hotel. They might have CCTV footage of that hallway."

"Are you telling me how to do my job?" he growled.

"I wouldn't dream of it." I was guessing this wouldn't be a good moment to ask him to share whatever he found when he reviewed the tape. Not that I really needed to know, of course, because I was *definitely* staying out of this investigation from now on.

He stood up, his face like thunder. "Well, thank you *very much* for your information, Miss Carter."

I stood, too, and he gestured for me to lead the way back to the foyer. Would he even look into what Travis had been doing? Or was he too annoyed with me to take my information seriously?

"I really am sorry about the crime scene, Detective," I

said over my shoulder. "It was just a spur of the moment thing. I only had a second to decide what to do." And it really had seemed, in that moment, that it would be better to know what Travis was up to inside room 428. Surely, he would look into it. He was a good detective, even if he had a quick temper.

I stepped back into the foyer. This time, Curtis was there; I spotted him right away. And with him— What was *she* doing here?

Kelly.

As usual, she looked like she'd just stepped off the runway, making me very conscious of my plain exercise clothes and the dirty paw prints where Rufus had jumped up on me. She was wearing an elegant ivory shift dress, her blond hair piled on top of her head in an effortlessly chic style. Her makeup was the sort that men thought of as "natural beauty", though in reality it took a lot of time and skill to apply.

Curtis was holding a stack of papers, as if she'd just given them to him. Was it something to do with the custody case? I couldn't see any other reason she would be seeking him out. They barely spoke to each other these days.

"Do me a favour, Miss Carter," Detective McGovern said. "And next time you're confronted with such a decision, choose to stay on the right side of the law." He wasn't yelling, but he made no attempt to lower his voice. Curtis and Kelly both turned to me, he in surprise, and she with a gleam of interest. McGovern stepped closer, looming over me. "If I find you interfering in this investigation again, I *will* charge you with obstruction."

He turned on his heel and stomped off. In the sudden quiet, the officer behind the desk shuffled some papers, trying to look busy.

"What was that about?" Curtis asked. He looked harried, but he'd looked like that from the moment I'd entered the foyer, so I didn't think it was on my account.

"Isn't it obvious?" Kelly purred before I could answer. "Your new girlfriend wants to get herself in the papers again. She thinks she's soooo clever, solving all these cases."

I moved to stand closer to Curtis, shoulder to shoulder with him against her. Well, shoulder to armpit, I guess. He was a lot taller than I was, though Kelly came closer in her sky-high heels.

"I had some information about the case I needed to report," I told him.

Kelly's malicious little smile widened. "Oh, I'm sure the judge will be thrilled to hear that your girlfriend is a nutcase who interferes in police investigations." She shook her head mournfully. "Not really an appropriate person to have around a young and impressionable child like Maisie, is she?"

"Leave Charlie out of it," Curtis said, but he looked sick.

I felt sick myself. Kelly was only too capable of twisting this to make us look bad and herself better.

"*You* brought her into it," she said. "Let's see what the judge thinks, hmm? See you in court."

Then she waltzed out the doors without a backward glance. I watched her go with a sinking heart. Forget jeopardising the murder case. Had I just jeopardised Curtis's chances of winning custody of Maisie?

CHAPTER 12

I DROPPED RUFUS AT HOME AND HEADED UP THE HILL, TOWARD the headland where the Metropole kept watch over the bay. I'd promised to meet Aunt Evie for lunch there, which now seemed like an excellent idea. I could do with a hug.

Feeling sorry for myself, I strode into the dining room, looking around for a tiny lady with a big attitude. I found her at a table by the window, dressed with her usual flair in tailored grey pants and a very warm-looking white jumper. The only bit of colour in her ensemble was provided by a pair of large red earrings.

She stood up to kiss me, and I squeezed her tight. "You look cosy!" I said. "That jumper is so soft."

She stroked her own arm in satisfaction. "I bought it last time I went down to Sydney. It was on sale, too!" Typical. There were few things Aunt Evie loved more than a bargain. She eyed me as I sat down opposite her. "Are you sure you're warm enough?"

I shrugged off my jacket, still warm from the walk, and

brushed ineffectually at those muddy paw prints. They weren't *that* bad. "I'm fine. Though now I'm feeling underdressed." My black leggings and sneakers didn't quite measure up to Aunt Evie's stylish appearance, even without Rufus's "help". I should have changed when I dropped him home, but I'd been running late.

"If I had a figure like yours, I'd be showing it off, too," Aunt Evie said, pushing one of the menus on the table closer. "Speaking of my figure, let's order. I'm starving."

I quickly scanned the menu, and we both ended up ordering the soup of the day. It was hard to go past pumpkin soup on a winter's day—it was such comfort food. Aunt Evie had always made it for me when I was sick as a child, and it brought rich memories of love with its sweet flavour.

I sighed deeply once the waitress had left with our order.

"Something wrong?" Aunt Evie asked.

"So many things." I told her about the disaster at the police station, how I'd not only managed to enrage Detective McGovern but had also given Kelly ammunition to use against Curtis in his fight for Maisie. I was still upset. How had it all gone so wrong? I'd have to apologise to Curtis, but I hardly knew what to say.

Aunt Evie reached across the table and captured my hand in her small one. "First of all, Luke McGovern is an ungrateful boy who needs to learn to control his temper." I blinked at hearing McGovern, who had to be in his forties, referred to as a boy, but I guess it was all about perspective. When you were almost seventy-three, forty was pretty young. "You gave him an important piece of information, and I'm sure once he simmers down, he will see you were only doing your civic duty."

I wasn't so sure about that. I had the feeling that Detective McGovern was a grudge-holder. "Maybe."

She squeezed my hand. "And secondly, you have to stop assuming that every man is as bad as Will."

"Will?" What did my no-good ex-fiancé have to do with anything? "What do you mean?"

"Curtis isn't going to be upset with you or blame you for anything."

Oh ... "He doesn't have to. I blame myself enough for both of us."

"Don't be silly." She patted my hand firmly and withdrew as our coffees arrived. When the waitress was gone, she resumed, "You did the right thing going to the police station. Curtis knows that. You know that. Even Luke McGovern knows that. Part of McGovern's annoyance is probably with himself, because he knows that if he'd returned your calls, he would have had this information days ago. He's just taking it out on you. And no judge is going to listen to Kelly's silly rants and think it is anything more than sour grapes and jealousy that her lovely ex has a new woman in his life."

"Maybe," I said again, stirring sugar into my coffee and taking a sip.

From our table, we had a view of the circular pool outside. It was heated in winter, but only one hardy guest was making use of it, swimming short laps back and forth across it: a woman, whose brown arms and shoulders looked strong as she powered through the water. Aunt Evie followed my gaze, and we both watched as the woman stopped at the edge of the pool for a breather, turning her face up to the winter sun. I recognised her immediately.

"It's Yumi," I said.

"I wonder what she thinks of her husband stealing from a crime scene?" Aunt Evie mused.

"There's no proof that he stole anything," I said absently, still admiring those shoulders. She was quite a small woman, so when I'd seen her at the photo shoot, I hadn't realised what strength she kept hidden under her soft, feminine blouse. I'd love to have muscles like that.

Not that there was the slightest chance of my ever achieving them. I didn't mind walking, but gyms really weren't my thing. If only you could grow muscles by eating chocolate.

"Don't go playing devil's advocate for that man," Aunt Evie scolded. "He's got enough devil in him without your help."

That snagged my attention. I smiled fondly at her, Yumi's muscles forgotten. "That doesn't make any sense whatsoever."

"Well, he must have taken something from that bathroom," she insisted. "What else was he doing in there? You surely don't believe he trespassed on a crime scene in search of a whiff of perfume?"

"No." I took another sip of coffee, but it wasn't having any effect on my spirits. I still felt like curling up in bed and hiding from the mess I'd made. "But, at this point, I don't really care what he was up to. He could make off with a whole hotel's worth of complementary soaps and shampoos, for all I care."

"You don't mean that. You couldn't stand it if he was the murderer and he got away with it because Detective Grumpypants was too busy trying to pin it on that poor dead woman's husband."

The waitress returned with our soup and thick slices of sourdough bread. I busied myself spreading butter on the warm bread till she had gone. "Well, Detective Grumpypants has the information now, and I can only trust that he'll use it effectively. I just hope that telling him hasn't destroyed Curtis's chances of keeping Maisie. What am I going to do if he loses the case?"

The very thought made me feel sick. Little Maisie with her dark ringlets and big brown eyes, her sweet nature and constant chatter. I'd known her less than a year, and already, I couldn't imagine life without her. Curtis would be beside himself if Kelly took her overseas.

Aunt Evie pointed her knife at me. "There's only one thing you *can* do."

I paused with my soup-laden spoon in mid-air to take in the look on her face. "What's that?" I asked warily. I knew that look. It meant that Aunt Evie had A Plan, and I would be expected to carry it out, however outlandish.

"Solve the case first and leave Grumpypants with egg on his face. Again."

I sighed. "Even if I wanted to—which I *don't*—how could I? If I knew why Travis was really in that room, what he could possibly have taken ... But McGovern will never tell me, assuming he even finds out. What am I going to do? Ask Travis nicely?"

"Eat your soup," Aunt Evie said with a mysterious smile. "The Lord helps those who help themselves."

I shook my head but did as I was told. The pumpkin soup was delicious, rich and creamy, and my bowl was soon empty.

Aunt Evie pushed her chair back and gathered up her enormous handbag. "Are you done?"

"What's the hurry?" I stood up, hurriedly downing the last of my coffee. Normally, our lunches lasted much longer than this. We never seemed to run out of things to talk about—we lingered over our drinks and chatted until the waiters began to get impatient with us taking up a table.

"Things to do." Aunt Evie stopped at the cash register to pay, then led the way out of the restaurant. But instead of heading for the exit to the carpark, she opened the glass door that led out onto the pool deck. "Places to be."

I shook my head. The task of keeping up with the workings of Aunt Evie's devious mind was often beyond me. "What places would those be?"

"Hush." She marched purposefully, if inscrutably, past the row of sun lounges that were set out facing the pool, though her attention was on the water. Yumi was still there, powering up and down. She'd turn into a prune if she stayed much longer, but she showed no sign of stopping. Maybe swimming was what had formed those muscles. Perhaps I should take lessons.

Yumi was still the only swimmer out here, and a towel

and white towelling robe were neatly folded on one of the sun lounges, awaiting her return. Keeping one eye on Yumi, Aunt Evie dipped as she passed the lounge, barely breaking stride even as she dug into the pocket of the robe and came out with a keycard. With a sly glance over her shoulder at me, she marched on, to the door on the other side of the pool that led back inside the hotel.

"Aunt Evie!" I was so scandalised I could only hurry after her, casting about in horror to make sure no one had seen my aunt's casual theft. "What are you *doing*? You can't take that!"

She waited until we had gained the safety of the carpeted hallway before saying mildly, "I'm not *taking* it, just borrowing it. We'll give it back."

"But you—you can't—" I broke off, hardly knowing what to say as she led the way back to the lift lobby. When we got into a lift, I took a deep breath and fixed her with a stern look. "That's Yumi's room key. You can't just help yourself."

"How else are we going to find whatever Travis took from room 428?"

"Maybe it's not up to us to find anything," I said as the lift doors slid shut. "Isn't it bad enough that Kelly saw McGovern telling me off? He said he'd *arrest* me for obstruction. Do you want to add breaking and entering to my list of charges as well?"

"You always were a dramatic child," was all the reply I got.

When the doors opened on the third floor, I followed

her out with a feeling of impending doom. "What if Travis is in the room and you just burst in?"

"Don't be silly," she said mildly. "He's here for a conference. He'll be conferencing."

"Someone just *died*," I pointed out. "They won't be working anymore."

"The wheels of industry keep turning, my love, even when someone dies. They're probably working even harder, in fact, trying to work out how they'll manage her workload until they can train a replacement."

I shook my head. "How do you even know which room is theirs?"

I remembered watching Travis entering a room that was next to an ugly painting, but it turned out that there was no shortage of ugly paintings in this corridor. I couldn't have said which room was his.

"Someone mentioned it on Friday night," she said. "When everyone was milling around wondering where Travis and his family were."

I caught her hand as she stopped in front of room 328. The mention of family had reminded me. "Stop! Their son could be in there."

Aunt Evie had the audacity to roll her eyes at me. "For goodness' sake, Charlie, I'm going to knock first."

"What if he's got headphones on?" He wouldn't hear her knock and we'd be caught red-handed.

"What if he *hasn't*?" she asked pointedly. "Don't be such a Negative Nellie."

My heart was pounding a million miles an hour as we

stood there, though Aunt Evie looked completely unruffled. No one came to answer her knock.

"I never picked you for a criminal," I muttered as she pressed the keycard to the door. The click of the lock opening sounded super loud, but there was no one else in the corridor to hear it. We went inside and shut the door behind us.

"Stop fretting and start searching," Aunt Evie said.

"We don't even know what we're looking for," I grumbled. I stood with one hand on my chest, waiting for my heartbeat to return to normal, but my gaze was darting around the room all the same.

It was a typical hotel room. A king-sized bed took up most of the space. Housekeeping had already been in, so the bed was made, a plain white quilt smoothed over it and tasteful beige pillows piled on top. A painting above the bed showed a view of Sunrise Bay from the northern headland, with the long white crescent of the beach and an improbably blue ocean washing up against it. Two teacups sat on the desk, and a shopping bag from one of the dress shops in town was on the floor next to it. Otherwise, there wasn't much sign that anyone was occupying the room.

Immediately, Aunt Evie opened the wardrobe and began poking through the drawers inside. I watched her for a minute, shuddering. My imagination was providing an all-too-clear picture of the trouble we'd be in if Yumi appeared and found us pawing through her underwear.

Well, it would have to be Travis walking in, I guessed, since Yumi had no key to unlock the door.

I sighed, moved further into the room, and opened the desk drawer. The only thing in it was a folder containing information about the hotel. The bedside drawers were no better. One held a bible, and the other was completely empty.

I glanced out the balcony door. It was a beautiful day outside. The wrought-iron railing was painted black, its pattern ornate, and even from inside the room, I could see it would come up to chest height on me. Wrestling a reluctant woman over a railing that high would take significant strength. The killer must have taken Krystal completely by surprise, giving her only time for that one shrill scream before she hit the ground.

A small, round table sat on the balcony, with a chair either side of it. Presumably, all the rooms were furnished similarly. Had Krystal been sitting on the balcony above us, admiring the view, when the killer crept up on her? Or had he been sitting out there with her, and she'd had no idea that someone she trusted had such a terrible plan in mind?

Travis's face flashed before me. He was so outwardly charming, even though I was fairly certain the man underneath that smiling exterior was a bit of a jerk. Would he have seemed harmless to Krystal? Maybe she'd let him in because he'd come to discuss something about work. If they'd been on the balcony together, she would only have had to turn her back for a moment ...

I shook my head. All I could do was speculate at this point, because I had no evidence. Looking for evidence was why we were here.

As I turned away, something lying on the tiles of the balcony flashed in the sun, but it was only a piece of broken glass tucked against the side wall. So much for housekeeping. Or clues.

Aunt Evie was in the bathroom, apparently having exhausted the possibilities of the wardrobe. I walked in to find her shutting a drawer, a disappointed look on her face.

"Nothing," she said. "Although I'm not tall enough to check the shelf at the top of the wardrobe. Did you look there?"

"Yep," I said. "It could be in the safe." There was a safe inside the wardrobe, the kind with a number pad where you input your own four-digit code.

"I tried a couple of combinations," Aunt Evie said, "but I couldn't get it open. I don't suppose you know when his birthday is?"

I blinked. "His birthday? Are we buying him presents now?"

She snorted. "No, you ridiculous child. Because he might have used it for the code for the safe."

I rolled my eyes. Aunt Evie was enjoying this entirely too much. "No, I don't know when his birthday is. Funnily enough, it never came up in the two minutes we were trespassing on the crime scene together."

"So sassy." She sighed. "I must say, I'm disappointed. I really thought we'd find something ..."

"Incriminating?"

"Yes. But maybe that ridiculous story about wanting to smell her perfume was true after all."

"Maybe." But then what had he been putting in his pocket as he came out of the bathroom? And what was that odd, hollow bang I'd heard just before he emerged?

My gaze landed on the toilet. Well, more specifically, the cistern. The cistern was made of ceramic, and it was quite possible that the sound of the lid being dropped back into place could make a hollow thump.

I grasped one end of the lid and started jiggling, trying to lever it up.

"Oh, that's a good idea," Aunt Evie said approvingly.

The top came free with a rush, exposing the water and pipes within.

And something else, tucked under a pipe.

I shoved up my sleeve and gingerly reached in, fighting the ick factor of having my arm in a toilet. It was just the cistern. Perfectly clean water. You could drink it if you wanted to. Not that I wanted to.

I showed Aunt Evie what I'd found—a phone, sealed tightly in a Ziploc plastic bag. Her eyes were enormous, and her expression was what some might have called gleeful. Seemed she was beside herself with excitement that our illicit search had actually turned up something incriminating.

Because it had to be incriminating, didn't it? Why else would Travis go to such lengths to hide it? What was on this phone that he didn't want anyone to see?

I nearly jumped out of my skin when the screen lit up and the phone buzzed insistently against my hand.

A call was coming in.

CHAPTER 13

I STARED AS IF I WERE HOLDING A SNAKE ABOUT TO BITE ME, THE number of the incoming caller imprinting itself in my brain.

"Are you going to answer that?" Aunt Evie asked impatiently.

Her voice stirred me to life. "Are you crazy? Of course not!"

I hurled the thing back into the cistern with much less care than I'd used to extract it, then jammed the lid back on. Wiping my dripping hand on the seat of my leggings, I grabbed Aunt Evie with my other and dragged her from the room. I don't think I even breathed again until we were safely back in the corridor, striding toward the lift.

My hands were still shaking as we got into the lift, but I pulled my own phone from my pocket and typed the phone number I'd just seen into my notes app before I forgot it. Though that moment felt as if it would be seared into my memory forever, and the number with it, it was best to be safe.

"What are you doing?" Aunt Evie asked as we rode down to the ground level.

"Just recording that phone number."

If she'd been Rufus, her ears would have pricked up at that. She turned shining eyes on me instead. "So you're going to ring it?"

"I don't know." I tucked my phone back into the side pocket of my leggings. Who was ringing Travis's secret phone? Of course I wanted to know, but the spectre of Curtis's court case hung over me. "I've got it now, in case I do. Or so I can give it to Detective McGovern." That would certainly be the sensible option.

Aunt Evie made a disgruntled sound as the doors opened on the ground floor. Without saying anything more, she marched across to the reception desk, a *sweet little old lady* smile plastered on her face.

"Hello, dear," she said to the receptionist. "I just found this on the floor. One of your guests must have dropped it." She held out the keycard she'd liberated from Yumi's pocket.

The receptionist took it with a warm smile. "Thank you very much, ma'am."

Aunt Evie returned the smile with interest. "We wouldn't want some poor person to get locked out of their room, would we?"

The receptionist agreed that would be a problem, then Aunt Evie took my arm in a surprisingly firm grip, marching me through the hotel and out the back door into the carpark.

"We have to tell Detective McGovern," I said, hoping to head off whatever horrifying scheme she was concocting. I'd seen that sparkling look in my aunt's eye before, and it always led to mischief.

"Not so fast, young lady," Aunt Evie said as we reached her car. "You don't want to add breaking and entering to your rap sheet, do you?"

I stared at her over the roof of her little red car, indignant. "*My* rap sheet? The whole thing was *your* idea. I was just along for the ride." Although I was already quailing at the thought of facing up to Detective McGovern with this latest piece of information. How could I possibly excuse my behaviour?

She stopped digging through her bag for her keys and waved her hand dismissively. "Illegal search, then. I'm sure there's something."

I frowned. "So what are you suggesting? That we *don't* tell the police about something that could be a crucial piece of evidence in their murder case?" Imagine how impressed Curtis would be with me if he found out I'd done *that*. It didn't bear thinking about. "Withholding evidence is also illegal!"

Aunt Evie had found the keys, although, considering how much stuff she carted round in that ridiculously over-sized bag, how she managed to find anything was a constant source of amazement. But she made no move to unlock the car. "Then you're damned if you do, and damned if you don't. You'll just have to solve it. It's the only way out."

I folded my arms, feeling mutinous. "No, it's not. I could ring the Crimestoppers line and leave an anonymous tip. I could send McGovern a letter."

She sighed as she studied me. "Do you really think Detective McGovern can find his backside with both hands? Do you *want* Travis to get away with it? That's not like you."

"So you've already decided Travis is guilty? There's no proof that that phone has anything to do with Travis Klein." Admittedly, the circumstantial evidence pointed enthusiastically in his direction, but there was such a thing as presumption of innocence. "Or even the case. It might have been left behind by a previous occupant of the room."

Aunt Evie's sceptical look said she wasn't buying it, but she smiled. "In that case, there's no need to mention it to the police at all, is there? I daresay there's no law against having a phone in your toilet."

Honestly, this woman. "You're lucky I love you so much. Because sometimes you're *really* annoying." The breeze picked up, sending icy fingers down my neck. "Are we getting in this car or not?"

She considered for a moment, then shoved her keys back into the depths of her bag. "Not. Come on."

She started walking back toward the hotel, and I huffed a sigh of pure frustration. "Did I mention how *very* annoying you are? Where are we going now? To hold up the bar? Kidnap a few people, maybe?"

"Stop being such a drama queen. I thought we might speak to Greta."

Well, at least it was warmer inside.

Greta was the events coordinator for the hotel, a lovely middle-aged woman who Aunt Evie knew well. They'd spent a lot of time together last year organising the Yule Ball—the same one that had ended in the theft of an expensive necklace being auctioned to raise money for charity. The fact that I'd managed to solve the mystery of the necklace's disappearance from right under the noses of over two hundred other people made me one of Greta's favourite people.

When we appeared in her office doorway, she took off her reading glasses and came around the desk to give us both a quick hug. Her hair was swept up in a neat bun and her lipstick was fresh, as if she'd just reapplied it. Perhaps she'd just finished her own lunch.

"Hello, ladies. This is a lovely surprise!" She beamed at us and gestured to the two visitors' chairs in front of her desk. "Sit down! Would you like coffee or tea? To what do I owe the pleasure?"

I looked at Aunt Evie, wondering the same. She settled into one of the chairs, clutching her enormous handbag in her lap, and turned her innocent blue eyes on Greta. "I was wondering if anyone has looked at the CCTV footage of last Friday night. I assume the Metropole has some?"

"Yes, of course." Greta shifted in her seat. "It was one of the first things the police asked for. It was fortunate that Detective McGovern was on the ball."

I purposely avoided catching Aunt Evie's eye. Clearly, Greta didn't share Aunt Evie's unflattering opinion of him.

"Oh, why's that?" I asked.

Greta leaned forward with a confidential air. "We only keep it for forty-eight hours before we record over it. We've found that that's usually long enough to settle any disputes that might arise, and it's a storage issue, unfortunately. We can't keep it forever. Video files take up a lot of room, you know."

Aunt Evie nodded sagely, though I was certain she had no idea how large video files were. Or any files, for that matter. My aunt had many skills, but computer literacy was not one of them.

"It was lucky that the poor lady was staying on the fourth floor and not the third," Greta added, then checked herself. "I mean, not lucky for her. Such a dreadful thing."

"Awful," Aunt Evie agreed. "But why does the floor make a difference?"

"Well, because the camera that covers the third-floor hallway is broken."

A shiver ran down my spine. I hadn't even thought about our little spot of breaking and entering being caught on camera. Thank goodness the camera was broken—that could have been a problem.

"It was reported to maintenance a couple of weeks ago," Greta went on, "but they've been slow to fix it. We wouldn't have been able to help the police at all if she'd been staying on that floor."

I chewed the inside of my cheek, anxious. Had Detective McGovern acted on the information I'd given him this morning? Because it had been Monday afternoon when Travis and I entered the crime scene. If McGovern wanted to verify what I'd said, or perhaps see how Travis had managed to open that door, he'd need to be quick to request the footage. It would be wiped tonight.

"Have you seen the footage from Friday night?" Aunt Evie asked with a suspiciously casual air. "Do you have access to that sort of thing?"

"Oh, no," Greta said. "Only the security team and the hotel manager have access to it."

Aunt Evie deflated. "So you can't show it to us?"

"Why would you want to see it?" She spoke to Aunt Evie, but she was looking at me. "I know you found the necklace last year, and the Metropole will be forever grateful, but this is a *murder* investigation. I really couldn't share anything with people outside the investigation. I'm sorry, but—"

"It's fine." I interrupted before Greta tied herself in knots. She clearly felt bad about denying us, but I certainly wouldn't want her to jeopardise her job to satisfy Aunt Evie's curiosity. "It was just a thought."

"Surely, your security people have looked at it by now, though," Aunt Evie said. "They must have seen who went into the room to kill that poor woman."

"Actually, they had a lot of trouble retrieving it," Greta said, shifting uncomfortably in her seat. She was probably regretting being quite so welcoming now. "The whole system needs replacing, not just the cameras. At first, we thought there was no footage at all, but we called in a specialist, and they managed to clean it up enough to be useful. They only sent it to the police this morning."

So, the only copy of the footage was at the police station. And Detective McGovern certainly wouldn't share whatever he found with *me*.

CHAPTER 14

CURTIS'S SHIFT ENDED AT SEVEN, SO I RANG HIM AS SOON AS I thought he'd be home. I stared out my kitchen window at the night, listening to his phone ring, with the sudden horrible idea that he might be so upset with me that he wouldn't answer.

Before my imagination could take this idea and run screaming into the dark with it, he picked up. "Hey, how are you?"

From the background noise, I could tell he was still in his car.

"Fine. But more importantly, how are *you*? I'm so sorry about this morning."

"Don't be. It's not your fault McGovern's an idiot."

I blinked. That was unexpected.

Curtis went on. "He should be grateful to have a prime piece of evidence dropped in his lap like that, not going off on a rant at you about something that wasn't your fault. Does he think you would have trespassed on his crime scene if Travis wasn't in the act of doing it himself? The man's afraid he'll lose his job if you keep showing him up like this."

"I wasn't talking about McGovern." I pressed the phone to my ear, obscurely comforted by his hot defence of me. "I meant that I'm sorry I gave Kelly ammunition to use against you in the case."

"She can try. I doubt she'll get very far. The judge is going to be far more interested in Kelly and her situation than a mere girlfriend." He cleared his throat, then added hastily, "That didn't come out right—you're not a *mere* anything. But you know what I mean. Kelly has such a chequered history, I'm sure the judge's focus will be on whether she can be trusted with sole custody."

"I hope you're right."

"I am."

Was that a hint of doubt in his voice? It was just like Curtis to hide his own worries to alleviate mine. But at least he wasn't mad at me.

"Gotta go," he said. "I'm just pulling into Mum's driveway to pick up Maisie."

"Say hello to her for me."

He promised he would, and we hung up. I stared at the phone a moment, still unsettled. Even if Kelly didn't get anywhere slandering me to the judge, it certainly wouldn't be a pleasant experience for Curtis. I sighed. I couldn't wait for this case to be over. Even if the result was everything we feared, at least this terrible waiting would be over.

I started chopping beef for a stir fry, which instantly attracted an appreciative four-legged audience.

"This is not for you," I told Rufus. "You've already had your dinner."

He gave me a reproachful look. Didn't I know that he was starving? That the *tiny* portion of dog food I'd served him was barely holding his body and soul together?

"And Aunt Evie says *I'm* a drama queen." I threw the meat into the sizzling oil, and a lovely garlicky smell soon filled the kitchen. "You're even worse."

Rufus thumped his tail on the floor, still giving me that beseeching look.

I pointed my wooden spoon at him. "Don't give me those puppy-dog eyes, mister. You are the best-fed dog in Sunny Bay. You're not fooling me."

As I sat down to my solitary meal fifteen minutes later, the phone rang.

"Hi, Aunt Evie," I said around a mouthful of stir-fried broccoli. "What's up?"

"I just had a call from Greta." Aunt Evie sounded breathless with excitement. "You'll never guess what she told me."

"Fortunately, I don't have to guess, because you're clearly busting to tell me."

Aunt Evie ignored my sarcasm. "She was talking to Xavier after we left."

"Who's Xavier?"

"He's the manager of the Metropole," she said impatiently. "Apparently, Detective McGovern asked for CCTV footage of the fourth-floor corridor from Monday afternoon."

I put down my fork and sat back in my chair. "Well, that's good. That means McGovern took me seriously, even if he was mad. He is looking at Travis, at least."

"Yes, but that's not the best part."

I grinned at the excitement in Aunt Evie's voice. She sounded like a little kid on Christmas morning. "All right then, I'll bite. What's the best part?"

"Well, apparently Xavier asked her to pull up a seat and then they both reviewed the footage from Monday afternoon before they sent it to the police. Now we know how Travis got in."

"Oh?" My curiosity was piqued. "How did he do it?"

"He was quite brazen about it, actually. The camera shows him passing a housekeeper's trolley further down the corridor. The maid was in the room and didn't see him, but she had left her lanyard with her keycard hanging off the end of her trolley, and he took it."

"Very brazen of him." It hadn't occurred to me that the maids would all have keys that opened every guest room door. I hoped the maid in question didn't get in trouble. She was probably supposed to wear that key around her neck, not leave it dangling where opportunistic guests could help themselves to it. "He was lucky she didn't catch him. She must've noticed that it was gone as soon as she tried to open the next room."

"Well, he only needed it for a moment, didn't he?"

"I don't remember seeing a housekeeper's trolley in

the hallway." If I had, I might have realised myself how he'd done it.

"Oh, she was further down, in the other direction past the lifts. You wouldn't have seen her."

Rufus came and slumped at my feet under the table, and I rubbed his belly with one foot. "Well, that is pretty exciting. Maybe Detective McGovern will hate me just a little bit less now."

"Greta said she saw you and Travis go into the room, too, and come out just a couple of minutes later. But that's not the exciting part, either." She lowered her voice to a melodramatic murmur. "Xavier told her something *else*."

I rolled my eyes. "Go on."

"He also said that he'd finally seen the footage from the night of the murder." She paused, as if she were waiting for an imaginary drum roll. "And *no one* went into the room."

I frowned. "So ... the murderer must have been hiding in there for a long time?"

"No, you don't understand. He said he saw Krystal and Justin leave to go to dinner just before six, and then Krystal came back by herself a few minutes before nine and left again almost immediately. No one else went into the room at all until Detective McGovern and Justin appeared after the murder."

My frown deepened. "Really? There must be something wrong with the footage. Gretel said they had a lot of trouble with it—they must have missed a bit."

"There's nothing wrong with the footage." Aunt Evie's

exasperated tone suggested that she thought there may have been something wrong with my deductive reasoning skills, however. "She couldn't have fallen from that balcony, or any on that corridor—because she wasn't there."

I shook my head in momentary confusion. There was no denying Krystal had died falling from a balcony. But, finally, my brain caught up. "Then we've got the wrong room. She didn't fall from the balcony of her own room at all. The police have been searching the wrong room for clues to her murder. Room 428 isn't the crime scene."

So Detective McGovern didn't have to be mad at me anymore for entering it.

"Now you're getting it," Aunt Evie said with satisfaction. "But that leaves the question: whose balcony *did* she fall off?"

I knew the answer already. "Room 328 is right under room 428. Given where she landed, that's the obvious place." And that explained why the killer couldn't just leave her red shoe lying on the balcony where it had fallen. If she'd fallen from her own room's balcony, one of her shoes lying there wouldn't have looked suspicious. But leaving it on someone *else's* balcony was incriminating evidence. They'd *had* to get rid of it.

"But that's—"

"Yes. That's Travis's room."

CHAPTER 15

THE NEXT DAY DAWNED DARK AND GLOOMY, WITH FORBIDDING grey clouds hanging low over steel-grey waves. The wind was bitterly cold as Rufus and I walked into town, as though it were blowing straight off the Antarctic. The waves out in the bay had white caps, and even the seagulls looked cold, their feathers ruffling as they were buffeted by the breeze.

I was only too happy to reach Heidi's warm shop.

"Don't look at me like that," I told Rufus as I instructed him to wait outside for me. "You have a fur coat."

Toy Stories was a children's bookshop that also sold toys. Or maybe it was a toyshop that sold books. Either way, it was full of bright colours and interesting things to catch the eye wherever you looked, and certainly not the least interesting thing within was Heidi herself, who came out from behind the counter to hug me hello. Today, she wore jeans, fur-lined boots, and a striped jumper in every colour of the rainbow. Her trademark plaited pigtails came down from under a white beanie with a rainbow pompom on top. She looked like an explosion in a colour factory, but she made it look good—although her face was paler than usual.

"You okay?" I asked when I released her from the hug.

"Yes, of course," she said, giving me a puzzled smile. "Why?"

I shrugged. "No reason." *You look tired* was so often taken to mean *you look terrible* that I didn't probe any further. Goodness knew having to run after energetic six-year-old twins was enough to make anyone tired, and I didn't want to insult her. "I brought back your copy of *Madame Bovary*." I laid the book on the counter as I spoke, its subdued, tasteful cover at odds with the riot of colour all around.

She raised an eyebrow. "That was quick. Did you end up finishing it?"

I screwed up my nose. "Not ... exactly." I'd meant to, wanting to give it another shot since Andrea seemed to like it so much—that was why I hadn't given it back to her at the book club meeting on Tuesday night. Heidi had pressed me to keep it as long as I needed to, but my good intentions had been rather delayed by the release of a new dragon book from my favourite author. After gobbling that up, nineteenth century manners and morals had lost all power to entice me. "I'm just more of a fantasy girl. I don't think the classics are really for me. I feel kind of a fraud going to book club at all."

"There must be plenty of dead fantasy authors," Heidi said. "I'm sure we could branch out a little."

That was the one rule of our book club—that the author must be dead. It seemed an odd requirement, but as I was the newest member, I didn't feel I could argue for a change. And besides, we spent more of our meetings sharing gossip than we did discussing the books.

"It's fine," I said. "Really, I go more for the company than anything. Well, that and the fact that Aunt Evie expects me to."

Heidi laughed. "She's a hard lady to say no to."

"If you only knew how true that was. The things she drags me into!"

"Worse than book club?"

"Let's just say that if I end up in jail, you'll know who to blame. You'll never believe her latest escapade." I told her about how shamelessly Aunt Evie had swiped Yumi's keycard, and how we'd searched Travis and Yumi's room and found the phone hidden in the toilet. "I think he got it from Krystal's room after her murder, so I guess it must be hers?"

"But then whose was the phone that got smashed in the fall?"

I cocked my head. "What phone that got smashed in the fall?"

"Didn't you hear about that?" Heidi leaned on the counter with a confidential air. "Priya must have told me. When they moved the body, they found a phone underneath her. She must have been holding it when she fell. But it was all smashed up."

"So why has she got two phones?"

Heidi gave me a quizzical look. "I think the more

important question is, why does she hide one in the *toilet*? It's not uncommon for people to have a work phone and a personal phone, but the toilet thing is pretty out there."

I nodded. She certainly had a point. "And how did Travis know it was there?"

"And why would he take it?"

"The way I see it, the only explanation is that they're having an affair. How else would he know about this secret phone of hers? Maybe Justin liked to snoop on her phone, so she had to keep a separate, secret one for Travis to message her on."

Heidi looked thoughtful. "So why would Travis be so keen to steal it? If Krystal's room wasn't actually the crime scene, why didn't he just leave it there? No one knew about it. Taking the phone is theft, but it doesn't implicate him as the murderer."

"Oh, I think it does."

"Not necessarily." Heidi seemed determined to play devil's advocate. "If they were having an affair and using this second phone to hide that fact, then Travis wouldn't want anyone to find the phone and expose him. Especially if she's already dead. Then it would just be a lot of drama for nothing."

"Yes, but if they were having an affair, it automatically makes Travis a suspect. They might have quarrelled and she threatened to tell his wife. Or perhaps he'd tried to break it off and she was getting weird and stalkerish about it. He must have thought the risk of taking the phone was worth it to keep the affair under wraps."

Heidi nodded slowly. "And it's not just his wife who'd

be upset, is it? It would break old Mr Klein's heart, if he's as big on family values as you said."

"True. Although it's not very *family values* to throw people off balconies. I feel like his dad would be more upset about that."

Heidi sighed and began tidying a display of bookmarks on the counter. "I just can't imagine being so crazy about someone that you risk your marriage and your reputation in your family to be with them—and then you throw them off a balcony."

I shrugged. "Romances turn sour all the time. Although, admittedly, people don't usually resort to such drastic solutions to end them. Surely, there's more to it than just fear of having the affair exposed." I paused, turning over Mr Klein's emphasis on family values in my mind. "Mr Klein did just anoint Travis as his successor at the helm of the family company."

There was a thoughtful silence as we both considered that.

"Do you think that promotion might be enough of a motive, if Krystal was threatening to tell Big Daddy about the affair?" Heidi asked.

"Could be. The affair might disqualify him from being considered."

The bell over the door tinkled, interrupting our conversation, as Priya entered the shop. "You two look like you're planning mischief," she said.

Heidi chuckled. "Just discussing other people's mischief."

"The murder case," I added.

Priya's eyes lit up. "Did you hear the latest? Krystal Dendekker didn't fall from her own balcony after all."

"We heard," Heidi said.

Priya pouted as she glanced at me. "How do you find out this stuff? *I'm* the reporter; I'm supposed to hear what's happening before everyone else. Is your boyfriend telling secrets?"

"Of course not. Curtis is far too principled to do that. Greta told Aunt Evie, and Aunt Evie told me."

Priya shook her head. "You've got to love a small town. You can't even go to the bathroom without everyone hearing about it."

"And speaking of bathrooms ..." Heidi's eyes glinted with laughter as she glanced at me. "Tell her about the phone."

I filled Priya in, her eyebrows climbing as I spoke. "Where's this mystery phone now?" she asked.

I shrugged. "As far as I know, it's still there."

She made an impatient noise. "I can't believe you just *left* it there."

"Yeah, well, some of us are not as keen to get involved in petty crimes and misdemeanours as Aunt Evie evidently is. Bad enough that we even *went* into that room, without taking something as well." I didn't mention that the phone had rung while I was holding it. If Priya knew that I had that number in my notes app, she wouldn't give me a minute's peace until I'd called it, and despite Aunt Evie's insistence that I needed to solve the case to declaw Kelly, I wasn't sure I wanted to do that. Still, the whole thing was giving me a sour feeling in the pit of my stomach, because Aunt Evie was probably right.

Priya didn't look convinced. I could only be glad that *she* hadn't been the one with Aunt Evie at that moment. They would have egged each other on, and who knew where that would have ended? Priya had been known to skirt the edges of the law in pursuit of a story.

"Did you tell McGovern?" she asked.

I glanced down, feeling guilty. "Not yet. I know I should, but he's already so mad at me. I don't want to get Aunt Evie and myself into more trouble."

"What's he mad at you for?"

"For entering his crime scene when I followed Travis in the other day."

She tipped her head to one side, confused. "You followed Travis into his own room?"

"No, the other—the room we all *thought* was the crime scene. Krystal's room."

"But now we know that wasn't the crime scene, so he's got nothing to be upset about."

"I don't think it works that way. He's threatened to charge me with obstructing an investigation before—what if he follows through this time?" I was all for doing my bit to help fight crime, but not if I ended up a criminal myself.

A customer came in just then, clearly wanting to talk to Heidi. Priya and I stepped back from the counter and Priya lowered her voice. "Then leave an anonymous tip. Ring the Crimestoppers line."

"From my phone?" I shook my head emphatically.

"You must be joking. He'd trace it back to me straight away."

"Then call from someone else's. Look, there's still that old public phone down by the surf club. Use that."

That wasn't a bad idea. "Maybe I will."

"Good. I've got to run now, but I'm going up to the Metropole later. Got an interview with the Kleins. Do you want to come?"

I chewed my lip in indecision. On one hand, of course I wanted to. Aunt Evie's voice was still ringing in my head, telling me the only way to ensure my behaviour didn't negatively affect Curtis's custody case was to actually solve the crime. But on the other hand ... this wasn't a game. Detective McGovern was genuinely angry with me already, and I didn't want to do anything to jeopardise Curtis's chances. If I got involved and *didn't* solve the crime—or even if I did, honestly—I could make everything worse. Was I prepared to take that risk?

But someone was still walking around thinking they'd literally gotten away with murder. And there was no harm in just tagging along to an interview, surely?

"Sure," I said. "I'd love to."

"Great." She flashed her teeth in a warm smile. "I'll pick you up from your place just before twelve." She waved to Heidi. "See you later, I've got to run."

Heidi looked up from her customer long enough to wave to us both, and I followed Priya out of the shop. Rufus leapt up, wagging furiously, greeting me with so much enthusiasm anyone would think I'd been gone for days rather than just a few minutes.

Priya hurried down the street, high heels clicking on the pavement. Rufus and I turned in the other direction, toward home. Our path took us past the surf club, and I stopped at the lonely public telephone. It was a wonder it was still here. I hadn't seen one in Sydney for years; they'd been phased out when mobile phones became so ubiquitous. But here it was, and still in working order, which was another minor miracle. Even when I was a kid and they were more widespread, they were often broken.

I dropped my coins in the slot and dialled McGovern's number. If I rang some anonymous tip line, I didn't know how long it would take for the information to get to him, and he needed to act on this soon in case Travis moved the phone again.

I leaned back against the clear wall of the phone booth, listening to McGovern's phone ringing. A couple of kids crossing the street caught my eye, and I was surprised to find I recognised one of them. It was Brandon, talking to another guy who looked a little older. The other guy was wearing a puffer jacket and a black beanie pulled so far down I couldn't even see his eyebrows.

Heidi's words at book club on Tuesday night came back to me, about the boy she'd seen talking to Brandon outside the tattoo parlour on the night of the murder. Was this him?

McGovern's phone stopped ringing and clicked over to voicemail, which was a relief. I had no interest in talking to him in person; I just wanted to leave a quick message and run.

But as I was listening to the recording of his gruff voice

directing me to leave a message, it occurred to me that he would probably recognise my voice as easily as I recognised his. I almost hung up, but instead, I straightened my spine and deepened my voice.

"Hyello," I growled into the phone. "I heff important teep for you. You must look een cistern of toilet een Trevis Klein's room. You veell find somtink verrry surprisink."

And then I slammed the receiver down and took a deep breath, waiting for the adrenaline to stop surging through my veins. Rufus was looking up at me, ears pricked.

"What?" I said defensively. "Haven't you heard a Russian accent before?"

CHAPTER 16

It was just before twelve when Priya pulled into my driveway. I'd been watching for her, so I gave Rufus a quick goodbye pat and hurried out to join her.

"Seen much of Jack lately?" she asked in a casual tone as she backed out of the driveway. Maybe too casual.

"We used to have pizza together on a Monday night all the time," I said, "but he's been getting a lot of evening shifts, so we've missed the last few weeks. I saw him briefly when I got home last Friday night, but other than that, no."

Considering that he lived in the other side of the duplex, you'd think we'd see more of each other, but life was busy. Plus, Jack being a nurse meant he worked odd hours, so we were often coming and going at different times.

Priya said nothing, focusing on the road.

"Why?" I asked.

She shrugged. "Oh, no reason."

I rolled my eyes. Priya and Jack had been circling each other like nervous cats for months, each ready to leap away the moment the other made a move. I'd had high hopes when Priya had conned him into pretending to be her boyfriend that he might *actually* become her boyfriend, but their fledgling romance seemed to have fizzled out. The only lasting result from that deception was the ongoing coolness between Priya and her mother Amina.

"You like him, don't you?"

For a moment, I thought she'd pretend to misunderstand me, but she sighed and gave me a sideways glance. "I don't know. He seems like a great guy, but I barely know him."

"There's a good way to fix that. Ask him out."

"I can't do that. It would be, like, the worst cliché to date him for real now after pretending he was my boyfriend in front of my whole family. That sounds like the plot to a bad romance novel."

I raised a sceptical eyebrow. "Since when have you cared what people think?"

She kept her eyes carefully fixed on the road, but she squirmed in discomfort. "Sometimes I try to imagine introducing him to my family as my boyfriend *again*, and I picture their reactions … and it just seems easier to avoid him."

I turned to face her fully. "You've been *avoiding* him? Priya, that's crazy! If you like him, you're just cutting off your nose to spite your face."

"You sound a lot like Evie sometimes," she grumbled. "It's not crazy, it's just simpler that way."

"Sometimes we have to do hard things in order to get what we want."

It wasn't often that I came up against this side of Priya. She was usually so strong and determined, but I'd noticed that around her family, she could be a lot less confident, as if the habits of obedience she'd learned in childhood still stuck with her.

"No one would believe we were actually going out," she protested, in a half-hearted attempt at self-defence. "They'd think it was just another trick."

Ah, yes, the old "boy who cried wolf" dilemma. I was very restrained and didn't say anything about actions and consequences. Go, me. Instead, I said, "Especially your mum, right? How is she, by the way?"

The car climbed the steep hill to the top of the southern headland. "Well, she hasn't mentioned marriage or even tried to set me up with anyone all year. It's a new world record."

"That's good, then," I said. "Mission accomplished."

"Yeah." She blew out a long breath. "Funny how getting what you want doesn't make you as happy as you thought it would."

"She's still mad?" That was pretty impressive. It had been more than six months. I made a mental note never to annoy Amina myself.

"Not so much *mad*, exactly. I think I could stand that more easily. She's more … *disappointed*."

"Apologise to her."

"I have!" Priya threw me an exasperated look. "But things still aren't right between us."

I folded my arms. Maybe it was time for some home truths. "Try apologising without implying that it's all her fault and she brought it on herself." I eyed her as she stared straight ahead, frowning. "You haven't done *that*, have you?"

"I plead the fifth," she said as we turned into the Metropole's driveway.

I sighed. "So, who's your interview with?"

"Whoever I can get."

"Oh. I thought you had something arranged?"

"Nope." She pulled into a parking spot and flashed me a smile. "I was hoping having you with me might make them more open to chatting."

I gave her the side-eye as we got out of the car. "And here I was thinking you wanted me along because you loved me."

"Nope," she said cheerfully, slamming the door behind her. "Just using you for my own nefarious ends."

"Nice."

Walking in from the carpark, we had to go past the main dining room. The clink of cutlery and the sound of people chatting, accompanied by the most delicious aromas wafting out into the corridor, reminded me that it was almost lunchtime. My stomach gave a very unladylike rumble as we came in sight of the main foyer and the front entrance.

"Hey, look who it is," Priya said, drawing up short. "Your biggest fan."

Detective McGovern, clad in another one of his hand-knitted vests, walked through the front doors and strode toward the reception desk.

"Do you think he's here about the phone?" Priya asked.

"Maybe." He was pretty slack about returning calls, but he'd certainly had time to listen to my message. "But he's got a lot on his plate. He mightn't have gotten to it yet." It had only been a couple of hours since I'd left my anonymous tip.

"Let's see where he goes."

We loitered in the foyer, partly hidden behind a pillar and a large potted fern. I still felt horribly conspicuous. McGovern finished with the receptionist and headed toward the lift bank, but partway there, he caught sight of something outside and altered his path, disappearing down the short corridor that led to the pool area.

Priya grabbed my arm. "I feel a sudden urge to lounge in the sun. Come on."

We followed in the detective's footsteps and were soon back outside, the smell of warm chlorine assaulting our nostrils. I saw what had attracted McGovern's attention—Yumi was stretched out on a sun lounge, reading, snuggled in a blanket as well as her white towelling robe. In the pool, Travis and Brandon played an aggressive game of volleyball, accompanied by much splashing and hoots of derision.

They made the perfect picture of family happiness. Personally, I wouldn't have chosen water sports in the dead of winter, but I supposed it was important to keep teenagers active, and the water *was* heated. The way they were jumping around and lunging after the ball in an effort to outdo each other was probably helping keep them warm, too. Some of the locals swam all year round in the ocean—I'd seen them when I walked Rufus along the sand, all rugged up in my winter woollies. Clearly, they were made of sterner stuff than I was.

Priya pulled me down onto a sun lounge on the opposite side of the pool to Yumi.

"We look so sus!" I objected.

"So?" She raised one eyebrow. "It's a free country. We can sit here if we want to."

"Technically, the pool area is only for hotel guests," I pointed out, but she shushed me.

Detective McGovern loomed at the side of the pool in his rumpled suit, his back to us. "I'd like a word, Mr Klein."

Travis caught the ball and gave him an impatient look. "I've already made a statement, Detective."

"I have a few more questions."

Yumi looked up from her book.

Travis stared for a tense moment, then forced a smile. "Of course. I'm always happy to assist the police with their enquiries."

He threw the ball back to Brandon, dived underneath the net, and came up at the side of the pool, tossing water out of his eyes with a flick of his head. A few drops scattered McGovern's shoes, but the detective didn't move away.

Travis folded his tanned arms on the side of the pool and gazed up at McGovern. "How can I help you?"

"You want to get out?"

"This won't take long, surely." Another smile, more assured this time. Travis struck me as the kind of man who was usually assured—confident that people would fall under the spell of that smile, that Daddy's money would smooth his path wherever he went.

I didn't know why I'd taken such a dislike to Travis, other than the fact that I suspected him of hurling poor Krystal to her death, of course. He'd never been anything but charming to me. Perhaps he reminded me a little too much of my ex, Will. He'd had that same air of privilege, the veneer of charm that hid what turned out to be some pretty ugly depths.

Really, sometimes, the whole presumption of innocence thing was very challenging. Just as well law enforcement wasn't actually my job.

McGovern gazed down at him, then shrugged. "Suit yourself."

Brandon hauled himself out of the water on the opposite side of the pool and took a towel from the sun lounge next to his mother. He was surprisingly skinny, almost gaunt. Board shorts weren't supposed to be figure-hugging, but his hung off him in a way that surprised me. He started drying himself, watching McGovern with a scowl that suggested he resented having his volleyball game interrupted.

Travis kicked his feet lazily behind him, creating little eddies in the clear water. He seemed completely at ease. No wonder he was in sales—he had a lot of confidence. Someone who'd been sneaking into crime scenes should surely feel at least a *little* nervous at being questioned by the police. And someone who I was more and more certain was the actual killer should be even more apprehensive.

"I'd like to know where you were on Friday night at approximately five past nine."

"I already told you this," Travis said.

"Humour me. Tell me again."

Travis sighed, as if this whole thing were vastly inconvenient for him. "As I said in my statement, I went back to my room to make a phone call. Dad has this stupid policy of no phones at dinner, and I needed to check some things with a supplier."

"On a Friday night?"

"It wasn't Friday night where he was. Time zones are a thing, Detective."

"Ooh," Priya murmured. "Sassing the police. This guy's pretty full of himself."

"You're absolutely sure about that?" McGovern had his back to us, but I could picture the stony expression on his face, judging from that cool tone of voice.

"Well, I can't be sure of the *exact* time," Travis said. "I wasn't checking my watch or anything, but it was about then."

McGovern hunkered down at the poolside, elbows on his knees. "Well, that's very interesting, seeing as how that puts you at the crime scene at the time of the murder."

"I beg your pardon?" Travis wasn't smiling anymore.

McGovern glanced across the pool at Yumi and Brandon, who had frozen in place. "Krystal didn't fall from the balcony of her own room. It was *your* balcony she fell from. So, I'll ask you again, where were you at the time of her death? Because if you were in that room, I can only assume that you were the one who pushed her."

Travis's feet sank to the floor of the pool, and he stood up, running a hand through his wet hair. "I—"

"Dad was with me," Brandon burst out.

Travis turned sharply toward his son. McGovern only studied the boy in silence for a long moment.

"Is that right?" he asked eventually. "And where was that?"

"We went into town." Brandon's dark eyes met his father's. "We got ice cream from that shop down by the beach."

"Do you have anything to add to that, Mr Klein?"

Travis was still staring across the pool at Brandon. "No."

"Would you care to tell me, then, why you lied about being in your room?"

I happened to glance at Yumi then, and the look on her face shocked me. She was glaring at her husband as if he were the lowest form of scum. What was *that* about? She had a personal hatred of ice cream? I nudged Priya and directed her attention to Yumi.

"I don't think wifey is buying this story," she whispered to me.

"She must have believed him when he said he was in their room," I whispered back. "But then where was *she*? Remember, she was supposed to be lying down in their room because she had a headache." This was getting curiouser and curiouser.

Obviously, husband and wife both knew that was a lie —but it seemed Travis hadn't been truthful with his wife about his own whereabouts. And he probably still wasn't. Heidi hadn't said anything about Travis being at the ice cream shop when she'd spotted Justin and Brandon. I'd have to check with her.

Travis shrugged. He seemed to have recovered his poise, though his face was paler than before. Perhaps he was just getting cold. "As I said, I didn't check the time. Maybe the work call was earlier."

Travis seemed to have some real issues with phones. It was pretty clear by now that McGovern hadn't listened to my message about the phone in Travis's toilet yet. Wait until he did—his head would *explode*.

"You didn't say anything earlier about going into town for ice cream."

"Yeah, I thought that happened later, so it didn't seem relevant."

"Let me be the judge of what's *relevant*, Mr Klein." The exaggerated patience of his tone suggested that Detective McGovern was barely hanging on to his temper. "I'll need you to come down to the station and make a full state-ment, just to make sure nothing else has slipped your mind." He glanced across the pool at Brandon. "You, too."

Yumi had smoothed her expression. "My son is a minor, Detective."

"And either of you are welcome to sit in on his inter-view because of that," Detective McGovern said. "Perhaps there's something you'd like to add to *your* statement, Mrs Klein? Maybe the family memory problems are catching?"

"I won't tolerate disrespect," Yumi said, her mouth a thin, angry line.

"And *I* won't tolerate being lied to," McGovern replied. "All three of you need to think long and hard about your statements. This is a murder investigation, and lying or trying to hide things won't go well for you. No more omissions or convenient lapses in memory will be tolerated."

Yep, McGovern would have a cow when he heard about the toilet phone—assuming it was still there and Travis hadn't hidden it somewhere else by now. I felt an urge to go check on it, or to yell at McGovern to listen to his messages. How much time would he waste getting further statements out of Travis and Brandon, while the phone sat there, its possibly incriminating evidence undiscovered?

"Get some clothes on," McGovern said to Travis. "You can come with me to the station now. The rest of your belongings will be released to you once my crime scene team has been over your room."

Maybe Yumi knew about it. What if she made some excuse to get into the room again and moved it while her husband and son were at the police station, and McGovern never found it? Or he didn't believe my tip and refused to act on it?

Trevor frowned at McGovern. "What do you mean?"

"The hotel will provide you with a new room. Yours is now a crime scene."

Not that there was much chance that the police would find anything helpful now, almost a full week after the crime—a week in which Trevor and Yumi and who knew who else had been free to do anything they liked in that room.

The urge to act was making me feel twitchy. I wanted to leap up from the sun lounge and demand McGovern go look for that phone *right now*, before it was too late, and the only thing we had left was the number in my notes app.

Which could have been a spam call, when all was said and done. I had no way of knowing if that number I'd saved had anything to do with the investigation at all.

Unless I actually rang it.

I chewed my lip as Travis hauled himself out of the pool and grudgingly began to dry himself. I might as well admit, if only to myself, that I was fully invested in this case now. I was itching to know who'd made that phone call. But the spectre of Kelly loomed, her lip curled as she promised to tell the judge about Curtis's interfering girlfriend. What had I told Priya? *Sometimes we have to do hard things in order to get what we want.* Time to take my own advice.

My phone was in my hand before I knew it.

"Who are you ringing?" Priya asked as I dialled the number from memory.

"Don't know." Before I could explain, McGovern turned and saw us sitting there.

He scowled. "What are you doing here?"

"Working on my tan," Priya said as I raised the phone to my ear.

Probably nothing would come of this. Most people just said "hello" when they answered a call, without giving their name. Unless I recognised the voice, I'd be no better off. But my heart was pounding, and it wasn't because of McGovern's scowl.

"Were you eavesdropping?" he demanded.

Priya pretended to be confused. "Eavesdropping? If you're so worried about privacy, you probably shouldn't choose public places to have your conversations. I'm just sitting here minding my own business."

"See that you do," he said.

"Nice vest," she said, ignoring his unfriendly attitude.

He glanced down at himself, obviously thrown by the comment. "Thanks," he said in a much less hostile tone. "I made it myself."

At another time, finding out McGovern was an expert knitter would have diverted me, but I was too focused on the sound of the phone ringing in my ear. Across the water, Yumi pulled her phone from her pocket and frowned at the screen.

"Hello?"

I heard the echo of her voice in my ear a split second later and abruptly ended the call.

Our eyes met as she slid the phone back into the pocket of her robe.

CHAPTER 17

"WE SHOULD GO," I SAID TO PRIYA. I NEEDED TO THINK. WHY had *Yumi* been ringing the phone her husband was hiding? If it was Krystal's phone, she must know that no one would answer.

Travis and McGovern were arguing about clothes. Travis had just realised the implications of his room being declared a crime scene, and was insisting that he couldn't go to the police station in his wet boardshorts and a hotel robe. McGovern was equally insistent that he *could*, because none of them were getting back into room 328 until the police had finished with it.

Yumi was watching me, a faint frown creasing her brow, and I hurriedly turned away. Did this mean she knew about the hypothetical affair? Could there be some *other* reason she had the number of Krystal's secret phone, and the affair was all in my head?

"Go?" Priya repeated. "But this is just getting interesting."

"Show's over," I said, trying to nudge her in the direction of the door back into the hotel. "There's nothing else to see here."

Travis eventually conceded that he could borrow some dry clothes from his brother, and the Klein family headed inside, aiming for the elevators. Detective McGovern, after one last scowl aimed at us, strode after them, clearly determined to ensure they didn't sneak back into the forbidden room.

"Let's go see what the rest of the Klein family makes of this latest development," Priya said.

"Let's *not*. They'll find out soon enough, and I don't want to be the bearer of bad tidings again."

"Come on, don't be a spoilsport." She gave me a pleading look. Considering her eyes were the same beautiful brown as Rufus's, her pleading look was top notch. "The public has a right to know what's going on here."

"I'm sure you have enough already for the newspaper. Don't give me those puppy-dog eyes."

She sighed. "A lot of it I can't print, of course. The police get twitchy if you publish too many details of their ongoing investigations. I'm really after the human interest angle. The older Kleins' reaction to the news that their own son's hotel room was the scene of the crime would be perfect."

"Leave them alone," I said, channelling an Aunt Evie level of firmness. "They're already having a terrible week."

"You're no fun," she pouted.

"Let's grab a drink from the bar."

She raised an eyebrow. "A little early in the day for that, isn't it?"

"I meant a coffee." I took her arm and dragged her along with me, half afraid that she'd run off to accost someone if I left her alone.

In the end, someone accosted us instead.

No sooner had we settled at a table overlooking the view out to sea with our coffees than Yumi entered the room, scanning it as if she were looking for someone. When her gaze fell on us, she marched straight over, so clearly, we were the someone.

"Why did you call me?" She slid into a spare seat at our table, her voice crisp and businesslike. She'd changed into a loose floral dress that looked like it must have come from Stephanie's wardrobe.

"I—" Wow. No messing around, straight to the point. I struggled for how to answer her.

"I know it was you." She whipped out her phone and tapped the screen. A second later, my phone began to vibrate in my back pocket, and she gave me a triumphant look. "Well? I just called the number that rang me and hung up out by the pool. Why did you call me?"

Priya's eyes were alight. There was nothing she liked more than a bit of drama, and we had drama here in spades. She turned to me like a spectator at a tennis match, waiting to see how I'd lob the conversational ball back to Yumi's side of the court.

I took a deep breath. *In for a penny, in for a pound*, as Aunt Evie was fond of saying—though even for her, imperial currency was a very distant memory. "I know about

Krystal's secret phone. I know you called it yesterday about this time. Why was that?"

Yumi was a lot prettier than Detective McGovern, but the scowl on her face now rivalled his. "How do you know that?"

"Because I was holding it in my hand when you called. That's how I got your number. I rang you today to see who would answer."

Yumi gazed out at the view for a long moment. The sky was a clear blue, untroubled by clouds. I couldn't say the same for Yumi's eyes. Storms chased each other through them when she turned back to us. "Where is the phone now?"

"I couldn't say for sure," I hedged. I mean, it was probably still in the cistern of room 328, but Travis might have moved it. Interesting that Yumi herself didn't know. "Tell me why you called it yesterday."

She blew out a heavy sigh. "I don't have to tell you anything."

"Why does your husband have Krystal's secret phone?" Priya asked.

Yumi hesitated, glancing between the two of us. "I thought *you* had it."

"Never mind," I said. "Why did you call it?"

She moved as if preparing to stand up. "None of your business."

It looked like my guess of an affair between Krystal and Travis was spot-on. I took a sip of coffee to gather my thoughts. If the phone belonged to Krystal, why would Yumi call it when she knew its owner was dead? The only reason I could think of was that she was trying to locate it, because she knew its existence would reveal the affair and incriminate her husband. I wondered how long she'd known about the affair. Her direct approach to me suggested she wasn't the type of woman to sit passively by while her husband cheated on her under her very nose.

Priya, for once, was silent, which must have taken a mighty effort on her behalf, but she looked at me, waiting for me to speak.

As if I had any clue what I was doing.

"You lied to the police about your whereabouts when Krystal was killed," I said before Yumi could stand all the way up. She sat down again as I settled the cup back in its saucer.

There was a long pause as she gazed impassively at me, hands folded on the tabletop. She had beautiful nails, long and painted a deep burgundy colour.

"Yes," she said finally.

"Care to tell us why?"

"Brandon wanted to go back to his room and watch a livestream from some gamer he follows." Evidently, she had reviewed her options and decided to try a more cooperative tack. "These family business dinners are so boring for him, so Travis said he could."

"He's seventeen, right?"

"Yes. He'll be eighteen in November."

"So why did you bring him at all? Couldn't he have skipped the trip and stayed home by himself? He's old enough to look after himself."

"He's had a difficult year," she said, looking down at

her hands. "We made him change schools, and he's been very unhappy with us. But he was in with a very bad crowd at his old school and his results were suffering. We hoped the change would help, but I think we waited too long. He's been in trouble a couple of times with the police."

Priya leaned forward. "What kind of trouble?"

She turned her face to the window. "The kind that comes in a little plastic bag."

"Dealing?"

"No." She shook her head sadly. "Just possession. But that was bad enough."

Wow. I bet old Mr Klein would have a cow if he knew his only grandchild was experimenting with drugs. That wouldn't fit at all with his vaunted family values.

"So you see why we couldn't leave him home alone. I wanted to get a single bed in our room for him, but Travis insisted that a seventeen-year-old boy needs his privacy, so I let him book a separate room for Brandon. Right across the corridor from ours." Her mouth tightened. "I made sure that I had a key to it. When we came back from dinner, I went to check on him. He wasn't there."

"Where was he?" I asked, though I already knew the answer. Hanging out by the tattoo parlour with Justin, of all people.

She looked at me then, and she looked so tired my heart went out to her. "He said he went to the ice cream parlour in town. But he was gone for hours. I know he went to get drugs. He was high as a kite when he finally showed up."

"So, you went to look for him?"

"No. I waited in his room for him to come back." She looked down at her clasped hands. "Please, I don't want him to get dragged into this mess. He's just a boy. Wherever he went, I know he had nothing to do with Krystal's death."

So Yumi still had no alibi. Though I felt sorry for her struggles with her son, I still hadn't let go of the idea that she might have more to do with Krystal's death than she was letting on.

"I think he's already been dragged into it," Priya said. "Or jumped in with both feet, more like. Why did he say he was at the ice cream shop with his dad?" She glanced at me. "I think we all know that's a lie, and it won't take the police long to figure that out, either."

"Brandon cares about his dad," she said carefully. "He's just a kid. Impulsive."

"You seemed ... upset," I said, "when you realised earlier that Travis wasn't in your hotel room."

Her mouth tightened. "He *said* he was going there, to call a client. He was unlocking the door when I went into Brandon's room. But he must have left afterwards."

"He didn't tell you that?"

"No."

"Where do you think he was?" I asked.

She shrugged. "I don't know."

"So maybe he *did* stay in your hotel room, and he's the one who threw Krystal off the balcony."

That would explain why Brandon had lied—he knew his father had done something and needed an alibi.

Although it didn't explain why Justin had lied about his whereabouts in the first place. Had he also been in search of drugs? What was it with all these people lying? I bet Travis's interview at the police station wasn't going too well, since Detective McGovern also knew that it had been Justin, not Travis, with Brandon near the ice cream shop, courtesy of Heidi's information. A whole bunch of truth bombs were probably detonating around Travis right now, and he wouldn't know which way to duck.

She fixed me with an icy glare and stood up. "How dare you? He would never do that."

"Why not? Is he a particular friend of Krystal's?"

The question hung in the air, holding her in place. Her lip curled ever so slightly. "They had a good working relationship," she ground out.

Was she still trying to protect her husband's reputation, even after he'd cheated on her? Or was she protecting him because *she* was the one who'd thrown Krystal off the balcony? She had those strong swimmer's arms, after all. I bet she could have done it. And I was more and more certain that Travis and Krystal had been having an affair, even if Yumi wouldn't admit it.

"Did anyone see you in Brandon's room that night?" Priya asked.

"No," she snapped. Hostility radiated off her.

I sighed. "Did you get on with Krystal?"

Yumi folded her arms. "Look, I know you think you're some kind of great detective. My father-in-law has told everyone the story about how you found the missing necklace last year. But our family is having a tough time.

I've been straight with you about Brandon's problems, but clearly, all you care about is yourself. This isn't a game. Don't ring me again." She pointed at me, stabbing the air with her finger as if she wished she could stab me instead. "Leave our family alone."

CHAPTER 18

I WAS STILL THINKING ABOUT MY CHAT WITH YUMI LATER THAT day as I headed into Sunny Bay's tiny supermarket to pick up a can of tomatoes I'd forgotten on my last big shop in Waterloo Bay.

She hadn't come out and said it, but I was pretty much one hundred per cent sure now that Travis and Krystal had been having an affair. I'd been fairly certain, given the whole phone-in-the-toilet thing, but the way Yumi had carefully skated around my questions had confirmed it. Poor Mr Klein. His family-friendly weekend had turned out anything but, though I doubted he knew about his son's infidelity. One more thing to add to the list, along with his grandson's adventures with illicit substances. That would be a shock, too.

None of this looked good for Travis. Had throwing his lover off the balcony been his way of ending the affair? Or had Yumi taken matters into her own hands quite literally, and gotten rid of her rival herself? We only had her word that she'd been sitting alone in her son's bedroom while the murder was taking place. Perhaps she'd told us that so we'd feel sorry for her and look elsewhere for the killer.

I actually did feel sorry for her, despite the unpleasant way our little meeting had ended. I knew what it was like to find out the man you loved had been cheating on you, so my heart ached for her. But my sympathy didn't blind me to the fact that one or both of them could still be guilty of murder. And it was surely only a matter of time before all the sordid details came out. Detective McGovern might have his failings, but he was nothing if not thorough.

Once he found that secret phone, it wouldn't take him long to put two and two together. And depending on how badly Travis's interview this morning had gone, he might already be in possession of all these facts.

I was lost in these thoughts as I approached the council carpark behind the supermarket. I'd walked down, but I'd left Rufus at home since I'd be going into the supermarket and he'd already had a big walk today. He hadn't even made much protest at being left behind, merely raising his head to watch me open the door, then settling back down with a sigh.

School had finished not long before, so I'd passed several kids in uniform chatting with their friends or going into Heidi's shop. There would probably be a few more inside the supermarket, grabbing chocolates or other snacks to fuel them on their walk home.

A young guy wearing a baggy jacket and a beanie pulled down low on his forehead was hanging around the big industrial bins at the back of the carpark. He was too old to be a school kid, but only just. Was it the same guy I'd seen with Brandon the other day? I thought it might be.

I stopped a good distance away, half hidden behind one of the parked cars, and snapped a photo of him, then texted it to Heidi.

Is this the guy you saw talking to Brandon on the night of the murder when you stopped for ice cream?

Her reply came back straight away. *Yep.*

Interesting. Was he waiting for someone? Brandon, maybe? I walked more slowly, keeping him in my peripheral vision.

A car horn tooted, and I turned toward the sound. A woman in a convertible was waiting to turn into the driveway of the council carpark, but the old lady crossing it on the footpath wasn't walking fast enough for her liking. The old lady gave her an icy look but didn't say anything. She may have even slowed her pace. I could almost see the steam rising from the impatient driver's ears.

Who turned out to be Kelly, because of course Curtis's ex-wife was the centre of the universe and no one had the right to slow her down even by two seconds. She was wearing dark sunglasses and a slash of bright red lipstick. Sitting next to her was a familiar curly-haired moppet. Maisie was dressed in her school uniform, her sweet face turned up toward her mother as she chattered—probably about something that had happened at school, since clearly, Kelly had just picked her up from there. Though they shared custody, Kelly had Maisie a lot more than Curtis did. He was only entitled to every second weekend, though he got her more often when Kelly was travelling for work.

It gave me a pang of anxiety to see Maisie in the front seat of the convertible. Since my accident, I'd been more aware of car safety than I used to be, and having a tiny thing like Maisie in such close proximity to the passenger side airbag worried me. The airbag going off in my own accident had most likely saved my life, but airbags were designed for adults, not children. They could do more harm than good when a child was involved.

I sighed as I watched the old lady finally clear the driveway and Kelly rev the engine aggressively as she turned into the carpark. Kelly's car had no back seat, so I understood that Maisie *had* to sit in the front, but it was just so typical of Kelly to choose her car based on looks and her own image rather than what would be safest for driving her child around.

Hopefully, after Monday, it wouldn't matter anymore. Curtis would win full custody, Kelly would jet off to Europe, and we'd all live happily ever after. Or something like that.

I was smiling to myself at the picture I'd just created, only half watching the convertible slide through the carpark like a shark, when I realised that Kelly wasn't parking. She'd done a loop of the carpark and drawn her car to a stop beside the big skip bins, which was a no-parking zone. Typical Kelly.

The guy I'd thought might be waiting for Brandon pushed off the wall he was leaning on and strolled casually in her direction. He didn't look like the kind of guy that Kelly would even acknowledge in public, much less speak to. They clearly moved in different circles. But Kelly spoke to him as if she knew him, and he nodded, pulling something from his back pocket.

Surely, he wasn't—? They weren't—?

They *were*. Right in front of Maisie, too. I couldn't believe it. My phone was still in my hand. Heart beating fast, I sank down even further behind the car I was standing next to and lifted my phone. *Tap*. My finger hit the shutter button as he offered her a small plastic bag. *Tap* again as she fumbled some money out of her handbag and handed it across. *Tap tap tap*, zooming in as much as I could on the transaction.

Was she *mad*? There'd been some talk last year that Kelly might be using again. Curtis had been concerned for Maisie's safety, but it had all blown over. Kelly's career was on the up and up. The jobs flowed in, she'd met this guy she was moving to Europe for, and her life seemed to be always improving, leaving her dark past behind.

Yet here she was, in broad daylight, buying drugs from some kid in the middle of downtown Sunny Bay. With her child in tow. She must be certain that she had sole custody already in the bag, that she was about to get everything she wanted. With so much riding on the outcome of the hearing, anyone else would have made sure to keep their behaviour squeaky clean, but not Kelly. She was already celebrating.

Was it because of me? Because she thought that scene in the police station tipped the scales so far in her favour that there was no way she could lose? Or was she so addicted that she couldn't think it through? I watched in horror as she drove off, transaction complete, Maisie waving goodbye to the guy as they went. Unbelievable.

Maisie looked happy, as if she were having the time of her life. I knew she liked riding in her mum's "princess car", as she called it. What did *she* think had just happened? She was only seven, but she was a bright kid. Why would Kelly take the risk that Maisie would tell someone? Her dad was a policeman, for heaven's sake.

I shook my head in disbelief, still reeling. But as I entered the supermarket to buy my tomatoes for that same policeman's dinner tonight, a new emotion began to take over. Outrage faded, replaced by a trembling hope.

I stopped in the middle of the canned goods aisle and pulled my phone back out. Quickly, I emailed the photos I'd just taken to myself, my fingers shaking with adrenaline. I wasn't taking any risks. If I somehow lost my phone or broke it between here and home, I would still have them. There was no way I was losing these photos.

Kelly had just handed us the key to winning the custody case.

CHAPTER 19

MY STEPS SLOWED AS I APPROACHED THE SURF CLUB. I WAS almost home, and I had a perfectly good coffee machine in my own kitchen … but the little café tucked into the side of the surf club building made the best coffee I'd ever tasted. And I felt I deserved a treat.

The umbrellas that shaded the tables outside were all closed, the chairs stacked away. The café would be closing soon, but the delicious aroma of coffee swelled out to greet me as I ducked inside.

What a week it had been. I ordered my latte with an absent smile for the barista. My thoughts were still in a whirl, full of Kelly and Curtis and Maisie, and what the photos I'd just taken would mean for us all. I stared out at the view of the ocean as I waited for my drink, nibbling at my lower lip uncertainly. Curtis needed to see these photos, but sending them in a text just seemed so … abrupt. I knew he'd be upset, and it seemed kinder to break the news in person that his ex was taking his seven-year-old daughter with her to buy drugs.

I'd only just made it out the door with my coffee in hand when two people heading toward the café from the beach hailed me.

"Hi!" said Stephanie Klein. She had Donal with her, both of them rugged up in jackets and scarves, their cheeks flushed from exercise and the bite of the sea breeze. Donal had a beanie on his balding head as extra protection from the cold. "How are you? Is that a coffee? I hear the coffee from this place is supposed to be good."

"The best in Sunny Bay," I said with a smile. "Maybe the whole world."

Donal laughed. "That good? That settles it, we're getting coffee."

Stephanie nodded. "I need something to warm me up after that walk. It's cold down on the beach."

"Pretty, though," Donal added, as if he thought I might be offended. "You're lucky to live in such a nice place."

"Trust me, I know." I took a sip of my latte, the rich creamy taste delighting my tastebuds.

"We just had to get out of the hotel," Stephanie added, her smile fading. "I suppose you've heard about Travis's room being where the murder happened?"

"Yeah, I did."

Stephanie sighed. "Poor Mum's beside herself. Dad's threatening to sue, though I don't think even he knows *who* he would sue. You can't exactly sue the police for investigating a murder, can you?"

Donal shrugged. "He's worried about the good name of the firm. It's understandable."

Stephanie rolled her eyes. "You'd think he'd be more worried about his son—or his dead assistant, for goodness' sake—than losing business, but that's Dad for you. Travis has always been the golden boy. Dad wouldn't believe for a minute that his precious boy could murder anyone—even though he *and* Yumi *and* Brandon were all lying about their movements that night. He thinks it's all a silly misunderstanding that will blow over soon."

"Do you?" I asked. "Think that Travis is the murderer?"

She gave a bark of laughter. "As if! The police are wasting their time investigating him. Travis is all flash, no cash. Well, you could say the same for all of us with the rates Dad pays, I suppose." She shared a rueful grin with Donal before continuing. "But Travis? He could charm the birds out of the trees, but do something that takes guts? Nope. Not happening."

"That's a bit harsh," Donal said. He gave me an apologetic look. "Siblings, you know. They say the worst things about each other. Makes me glad to be an only child."

Stephanie snorted. "You think it's harsh of me to say my brother's not capable of murder?"

"I hope he has a good lawyer," I said. "The evidence is starting to add up."

"Do you think so?" She seemed to have forgotten all about that coffee. "Now, if they were questioning *Yumi*, I'd be more inclined to believe it."

"You don't like Yumi?"

"She's okay. We're not best friends or anything, but there's nothing *wrong* with her. She's just ... a more forceful personality. Got more of a spine than Travis. She can be ruthless when she wants to be."

I glanced at Donal, but he looked away, as if he wished this conversation weren't happening. I noted that he wasn't leaping to Yumi's defence, though. "Ruthless in what way?"

"She's kind of a *my way or the highway* person. She's very polite about it, but I wouldn't want to get on her bad side. And we only have her word for it that she was waiting in Brandon's room for him to come home, don't we? It wouldn't surprise me if the story changed again."

Now Donal did protest. "You can't go around accusing people. Next you'll be saying your father did it."

Stepanie rolled her eyes. "You know perfectly well he was with us at the restaurant. But nobody saw Yumi. She could have done it."

I certainly wasn't going to argue the point, since I'd been thinking the same thing. As far as I was concerned, both Yumi and her husband were still suspects, and I hadn't even decided yet which one I thought the more likely of the two. I needed more information.

"I thought we came out for a walk to get away from all the talk of the investigation," Donal gave me an apologetic glance. "I'm sure you're not interested in hearing all our family dramas."

"Of course she is," Stephanie said before I could answer. "The whole town's talking about it." She shook her head. "What a mess. No one will ever hire Klein's World of Kristmas again."

"I'm sure that's not true," I protested.

"Come on. Would you order happy Christmas elves and dancing reindeer from a family of murderers?"

"Steady on there," said a new voice.

I turned to find Angus and his wife Delphine approaching. It looked as though everyone was keen to escape the confines of the hotel. It was Angus who had spoken, and he was giving his sister a look that was half annoyed and half amused.

"Be careful who you're calling murderers," he said. "Some of us had nothing to do with it."

Some of us weren't at the table when I went to the restaurant, though. *Some of us* had walked in on my heels and might have had time for a quick spot of murder.

"*All* of us had nothing to do with it," Delphine said firmly, smiling up at her husband. She had her arm tucked through his, the picture of domestic happiness. "It will probably turn out to be one of the staff, and this will have all been a fuss about nothing."

I blinked. A woman was still *dead*. I'd hardly call that a fuss about nothing. "I'd better get going," I said, holding up my bag of tomatoes as evidence. "I've got to get home and start cooking."

"You need to go back," Angus said to Stephanie. "Mum's a mess."

"I'll have my coffee first," she said as I started to back away. "Mum can wait."

"You haven't heard," he insisted. "It all hit the fan after you two left."

I paused, caught by the odd excitement in his tone, and took another sip of my cooling coffee to delay my exit.

Stephanie gave him a suspicious look. "What's happened now?"

"The police found a phone hidden in Travis's room. You'll never guess who it belonged to."

"Krystal," I said automatically. I couldn't help myself. Thank goodness Detective McGovern had finally found the phone.

Angus gave me a dirty look, annoyed to have his thunder stolen. "That's right. Travis just confessed that he and Krystal were having an affair."

I was torn between pride at being right and shock that Travis had actually come out with it.

"I thought your father would have a heart attack when he heard," Delphine said, her eyes shining with the same suppressed excitement that was in her husband's.

Angus nodded. "You know what he's like."

Yes, we all knew how important family values were to Robert Klein. Probably the whole of Sunny Bay knew by now. It must have been a terrible blow to find out his supposedly happily married son was having an affair.

"But it's good news for Angus, isn't it, darling?" Wow. Delphine couldn't even *pretend* to be upset. "Robert won't want someone like that at the helm of his company. Now the job will go to someone who really deserves it, just like it always should have."

Now I knew why Yumi had tried to keep the affair

quiet. She must have known that it would cost Travis his promotion if word got out.

Angus nodded, a smug smile on his face. "The best man for the job."

I looked at their smiling faces and suspicion stirred. The timing of Angus's absence from dinner *had* been mighty convenient. Could he have killed Krystal to frame Travis and get him out of the line of succession? He wasn't exactly distraught about his brother's downfall. But surely, that was too extreme. If Angus was prepared to kill for a promotion, why not kill Travis himself? Why drag poor Krystal into it?

I had to wonder—was being the boss of Klein's World of Kristmas *really* such a prize that people would kill for it?

CHAPTER 20

RUFUS WAS ALREADY WAITING AT THE DOOR, WAGGING UP A storm, before Curtis rang the doorbell. Before Curtis even got out of his car, actually. He knew the sound of Curtis's engine, so as soon as the big car pulled into the driveway, he knew one of his favourite people in the world had arrived.

The feeling was mutual. As soon as I opened the door, Curtis crouched down to give the scritches behind the ears and vigorous pats that Rufus so delighted in.

"Who's a good boy?" he asked, beaming as Rufus's tail hammered against the wall. "Is it *you*? Yes, it *is*. Rufus is a *good boy*, aren't you?"

Curtis had changed out of his uniform and was wearing jeans and a cream cable-knit sweater that made him look like a fisherman ready to wrestle the waves in his trawler. Or, at least, a model version of a fisherman, with strong hands and a sexy five o'clock shadow on his square jaw but without the gross fishy smell.

"I've been a good girl, too," I said, smiling down at the pair of them fawning all over each other. "In case you're interested."

He stood up then, looming over me, and folded me into his arms. "Hello to you, too."

"Good to know that the dog is a higher priority than me." I snuggled into the soft wool of his sweater, breathing in the sweet summer scent of his aftershave.

"Well, he *is* a very cute dog."

I drew back far enough to smack his arm. It was like smacking a boulder. Curtis was a big guy, and none of it was fat. His biceps alone were practically the size of my head.

He bent his head, and our lips met in a long, lingering kiss. I didn't think I could ever get tired of kissing Curtis. We'd been going out for just over six months, and each time I saw him, I still felt a thrill of excitement, as if we were meeting for the first time all over again. He always seemed taller than I remembered, more handsome, just ... more.

And that smile of his should be registered as a lethal weapon.

He drew back, and I finally got a chance to shut the door. Rufus, still wagging, led the way into the kitchen, where my pasta sauce had been simmering since I got back from the supermarket.

Curtis sniffed appreciatively. "Smells delicious."

"Let's hope it is." I gave it another stir. "I haven't tried this recipe before, so you're my guinea pig."

"I'm always happy to be experimented on."

I raised an eyebrow at him, and he grinned.

"Get your mind out of the gutter, young lady." He came up behind me and put his arms around me. "How was your day?"

"Funny you should ask, actually." I'd been busting to tell him this for hours, yet now the moment was here, I hesitated, unsure of his reaction. Then I gave myself a stern reminder that Curtis was not Will. Giving my ex difficult news had often led to tantrums and sulks and days of cold treatment, but Curtis wasn't like that.

I took off my apron and grabbed my phone off the kitchen counter. Swiping through my photos, I found the one I'd sent to Heidi, of the shady-looking guy loitering by the skips in the council carpark.

"Do you know this guy?"

He leaned closer, frowning. "Looks like Danny Vickers. Why? What are you doing with a photo of him on your phone?"

"What do you know about him?"

"He's been busted for possession a few times. Not the most savoury character. I hope he's not a new client of yours?"

I took a deep breath. "I saw him with Kelly this afternoon."

His curious smile flattened. "What do you mean?"

In answer, I scrolled to the next photo, showing Danny talking to Kelly. Then the next one, as something changed hands between them, with Maisie clearly in the shot in the front seat. Curtis held out his hand for the phone, then flicked back and forth between the photos, zooming in as much as he could on that exchange. His face was like stone.

"How could she?" He looked up at last, fury in his eyes. "I'm going over there right now to get Maisie."

I caught his arm. "No, don't."

He shrugged my hand off. "I can't leave my child with her. It's not safe."

"You can't afford to do anything to jeopardise the case. You know Kelly. If you go in there, guns blazing, she'll find some way to turn this around and make you look like the bad guy. She'll say you're denying her access, or accuse you of kidnapping or something." Anything was possible with someone who had such a loose relationship with the truth.

"But Maisie—" He broke off, turning away from me.

"This isn't a new thing," I said. "Maisie's been fine this long. I'm sure another night won't hurt."

I sent up a silent prayer that nothing would happen to make me eat my words. I loved that kid, and it killed me to think of her in Kelly's care. If you could even call it "care".

But the important thing here was to secure Maisie's future. She was no toddler. It wasn't as if Kelly could leave her to drown in the bath or something terrible like that. For a seven-year-old, she was pretty self-sufficient.

"Give these photos to your lawyer first thing in the morning," I urged him. "He'll know what to do so that everything goes through proper channels."

Curtis turned back to me, brown eyes hard. "Send them to me. Why didn't you send them as soon as you took them? Why wait until now to tell me?"

Behind us, the pasta sauce bubbled away, ignored. I took the phone and put the photos into a text to him. "I wanted to tell you in person. I knew you'd be upset."

"I could have sent them to Paul already."

"Could Paul have arranged a meeting with the judge at four o'clock in the afternoon?"

There was a tense silence until his shoulders relaxed. "No. I guess not. He couldn't even have made it to Sydney before the end of the business day." He stared down at the floor and blew out a long breath. "I'm sorry. I didn't mean to snap at you. None of this is your fault." Chimes announced the arrival of the photos, and he pulled out his phone. "I'll send them to him now. Will you excuse me a minute while I ring him?"

"Sure," I said, but he was already striding to the back door. He slid it open and stepped outside into the cold. Rufus followed, curiosity getting the better of him.

I turned back to the stove. That had gone about as well as I could have expected. Might as well serve dinner while he was busy. It was after seven, but I was confident Paul would take his call. He and Curtis had played on the same football team in high school and had remained friends.

The alluring scent of garlic tickled my nose as I plated up our meals and carried them to the table. I sat down, fiddling with the tablecloth while I waited. From where I sat, I could see Curtis striding back and forth, one hand clamping the phone to his ear while the other waved as he talked. When he came back in, he was a different man, his face aglow with victory.

I stood up, hands clasped tightly together. "Well? What did Paul say?"

A dimple peeked out as a smile lit his face. That dimple and I were old friends, but it was only now that I realised how long it had been since I'd seen it. "He says we've got her." Strong hands reached for me, and before I knew it, I was in the air, being twirled round and round.

"Put me down!" I batted ineffectually at him, laughing. "You crazy man. Oh, look out, Rufus! No, this is not a game."

Rufus didn't believe me. He thought it seemed like great fun, and kept leaping up, pawing at us both, wanting to join in. Chaos reigned, but I didn't care. I knew how much this meant to Curtis. He'd been weighed down by the fear of losing Maisie for the past few months, and it was a joy to see him relieved of that burden.

Curtis set me down, but he didn't let go, gathering me into a tight hug. "Thank you, Charlie."

"Don't thank me yet." I reached down to pat Rufus, trying to calm him, and scored an excited lick for my trouble. "The hearing isn't over yet."

"Paul says no judge in the world will award sole custody to a parent who is not only using drugs but takes their child along to buy them." He breathed out a shuddering breath, giddy with relief. "Maisie is safe."

He kissed me long and hard, and I melted against him. It didn't seem to matter how many times I kissed Curtis, it always left me feeling breathless. My appetite for dinner fled, chased out by a different kind of hunger.

"We should celebrate." His voice was husky, and a

wicked smile played around his full lips. He swept me into his arms, making me squawk in alarm. Rufus barked as he carried me toward the stairs.

"Stop!" I gasped. "I can walk." I had visions of us both tumbling down the stairs, particularly with Rufus still leaping about like a deranged Tigger, demanding to join the game. "This is police brutality!"

He smirked down at me. "Want me to get out my handcuffs?"

"For you or me?" I hid my face against his neck, breathing in his scent, until the peril of the stairs was past.

I felt his shrug as he shouldered my bedroom door open. "I'm down for either."

I opened my eyes again as he dropped me on the bed. "Get *off*, Rufus!"

Rufus had landed on the bed at the same time I did, hot dog breath in my face as he barked with delight at this new game.

"Down, boy," Curtis ordered.

It took a couple of tries, but Curtis managed to persuade Rufus to stay on the floor. The poor dog flopped down with a groan and put his head on his paws. That taken care of, Curtis took his place on the bed, his long body covering mine, propping his weight up on his elbows. His eyes were alight with mischief.

"What about dinner?" I asked.

"I'm looking at it," he said, and lowered his head to mine.

CHAPTER 21

I was up early on Saturday morning. The air was crisp and chill, but the sky was a brilliant clear blue, promising a glorious winter's day.

"You're lucky you've got a fur coat," I told Rufus as we headed down to the beach for a walk. I was snuggled into my thickest jacket and a pair of fleece-lined trackpants. After our walk, I'd shower and get dressed in something a trifle more up-market, but right now, warmth was the priority.

He ignored me in favour of the delights of the nearest telegraph pole. After giving it a good sniff, he lifted his leg so high that his balance seemed precarious.

"You're going to fall over one of these days doing that. You'll be trying to outdo some Great Dane, and next thing you know, you'll be flat on your back on the grass—and who's going to impress all the lady dogs then, hmmm?"

He galloped ahead down the stairs to the sand, and I followed more sedately, looking to see who was out on the water. A few surfers bobbed in the swell near the northern headland, little black blobs sitting on the waves. Closer in, a couple of paddleboarders scooted along parallel to the beach. No one was swimming. It was too late for the early morning die-hard swimmers, and too early for families bringing their kids down. In summer, the beach would be alive with people already, but not many braved the winter chill, although a few walkers were out, enjoying the peaceful morning.

A man was sitting near the high tide mark among a scatter of seaweed, contemplating the waves. As I drew closer, I realised it was Justin, Krystal's husband.

Rufus trotted up to him, tongue lolling from the side of his mouth. Justin broke his thousand-yard stare and turned to him, stroking his soft ears. Rufus sat down and slumped against Justin's side.

"Nice dog," he said. "Is he yours?"

"Yeah." I stopped and shoved my hands into my pockets to keep them warm. "He kind of adopted me when I moved into the neighbourhood."

"What's his name?"

"Rufus."

Rufus looked up at the sound of his name and bestowed a thoughtful lick on Justin's chin.

"I always wanted a dog," Justin said. "But Krystal was more of a cat person. I guess I'll be able to get one now."

I blinked. What an odd thing to say. But it wasn't a gloating kind of remark. He was just stating a fact, though the colourless tone suggested that the longed-for dog would no longer make him happy. I had a feeling that if he did get one, he would think of his lost wife every time he looked at it, and my heart went out to him.

"Want some company?" I asked.

"Sure," he said, still in that dull tone, as if he didn't care one way or the other.

I sat next to him. The sand was still cool, and the cold radiated even through my thick trackpants. Rufus flopped down between us, and Justin continued to stroke his soft head.

"Are the police keeping you up to date with their investigation?" I asked.

He glanced at me. "They don't think I did it anymore, if that's what you mean. Someone told them she saw me in town at the time of the murder."

At the time of the murder. He said it so calmly, as if he were talking about something that had happened to someone else, or the plot of a book we'd both read. Would I be able to discuss Curtis's murder so calmly? I guessed we all handled grief differently.

"That was my friend." I hesitated over my next question, then decided to go for it. When would I get another chance to talk to him? "What were you doing there?"

He shrugged without taking his eyes off the horizon. "Just going for a walk."

"With Brandon Klein?"

"Word gets around fast. I didn't go with him, I ran into him in town."

"Because he was introducing you to his dealer?"

That got his attention. His hand stilled, and the look he turned on me was suddenly wary.

"I know that guy Danny you met there is a local dealer. Did you tell the police you were there to see him?"

"No, but I guess they'll find out. Seems like it's hard to keep secrets in Sunrise Bay." Rufus butted his hand, and Justin resumed patting him, staring down at the dog as if he were talking to him and I wasn't even there. "You know, I keep thinking about that night. How if I'd been there, she'd still be alive."

Again, there was no emotion in his tone. He was just making an observation. If I wasn't a hundred per cent sure he couldn't have done it, I'd be wondering if I were sitting next to a murderer. Instead, I was worrying that he was in for a spectacular breakdown when he finally allowed himself to feel the emotions he had pent up inside.

"I saw you guys arguing in the bar." If it hadn't been for that argument, he wouldn't have stormed off into the night and left his wife to face her killer. "What was that about?"

"Just normal couple stuff," he said, but he was looking away again, and I got the feeling he wasn't being completely honest. "But I was so mad I needed something to calm me down." He rubbed the back of his neck with his free hand. "I texted Brandon to see if he had anything. I've … I've bought from him a couple of times in the past."

"This couple stuff wouldn't have been about the fact that your wife was having an affair with Travis Klein, would it?"

He sighed, and there was resignation in that soft exhale. Rufus dropped his muzzle onto Justin's denim-clad leg. "I guess everyone's heard by now."

"As you said—it's hard to keep secrets in Sunny Bay." Particularly when they had to do with a juicy murder case.

"Well, apparently, it had been going on for months, right under my nose, but I only got suspicious a few weeks back. I even got into her phone one day when she was in the shower, looking for texts from another man, but there was nothing there."

That would be because she'd had that secret phone for contacting her lover. In our brief interactions, Krystal had struck me as a highly organised woman, and she'd certainly organised her affair very efficiently.

That must have been what Yumi had done, too— looked through her partner's phone for texts from a lover. That was how she'd found the number of the secret phone. Travis should have taken a leaf out of his lover's book and gotten a second phone, too.

"But you were still suspicious?" I asked. "Why?"

He lifted one shoulder. "There were a lot of little things. Maybe by themselves, they wouldn't have made me suspicious, but taken together, they were pretty damning."

"Like what?"

"Like her having to spend a lot of late nights at work when she never had before. Like always being too tired for … well, you know. Suddenly, all this expensive jewellery started to appear, and I knew *we* couldn't afford it. I guess he was buying it for her. She said it was fake, but I'm not an idiot." He stroked Rufus's soft head pensively. "And when I met the guy, I could see he was just her type. Never pegged him for a murderer, though."

"You think he did it?"

He looked at me then, his expression bleak. "Who else?"

Travis did seem to be the most likely suspect, though I wasn't ruling Yumi out just yet. "So, is that what you were arguing about that night? The affair?"

He nodded. "I saw the way Travis looked at her at dinner that night, and I just *knew*. I knew I hadn't been imagining things. When we got to the bar, I confronted her about it. She denied it at first, but I told her I'd go upstairs and ask him in front of everyone if she didn't tell me the truth, so she did." He heaved another sigh. "They say you should be careful what you wish for. She told me she wanted a divorce."

Interesting. Had Travis been prepared to leave his wife for Krystal? Was he even aware that Krystal was going to ask her husband for a divorce?

Had *Yumi* known? I was already certain she'd known about the affair, but if she'd known it was about to destroy her marriage, did that give her a motive? Maybe. They say hell hath no fury like a woman scorned, but murder was a big step just because your husband was planning to leave you.

"So you argued, then went to buy drugs. Then what? You told Detective McGovern you were walking on the beach, but there was no sand on your shoes."

He snorted. "I'd just bought weed. What do you *think* I did?"

Fair enough. That wouldn't be something he'd want to

tell the police. "Why didn't you come back to the hotel to smoke it? Were you just standing around in the street?"

"You're relentless, aren't you?" he said, without any rancour. "I was still mad at Krystal and shocked she wanted a divorce. I didn't want to see her, so I stayed out for a while, just walking around, thinking. Then when that cop asked me where I'd been, I had to come up with something on the spot. I knew they'd think I did it, and I panicked. My mind just blanked. Walking on the beach was the first thing I thought of."

"Why did you think they would assume it was you?"

"Don't they always assume it's the husband?" He shrugged. "To be fair, most of the time, they're right. Domestic violence is a huge problem in this country."

That was true, unfortunately. "But not this time. You didn't do it."

"No, I didn't." Finally, some emotion entered his voice as he added, "I hope they lock that mongrel Klein up forever."

So did I, but first we had to figure out *which* Klein was the guilty party.

CHAPTER 22

I LEFT JUSTIN STILL SITTING THERE, GAZING OUT TO SEA, AND Rufus and I continued on to the surf club. I was meeting Aunt Evie there for brunch, continuing a tradition that we'd begun when I first moved to Sunny Bay. Sometimes, she was busy, or I had a client, but whenever we could, we got together on Saturday morning to discuss life, the universe, and everything. It was a fun way to start the weekend.

She was already there, seated at one of the outdoor tables despite the chill in the air, rugged up in a very stylish overcoat in an unmissable magenta.

"Is this new?" I asked as I kissed her perfumed cheek. "It's fabulous."

"Got it in the sales last week," she said, beaming up at me. "Isn't it gorgeous? So warm, too! I've already ordered you a latte." She pushed the menu toward me, though she might as well have ordered food for me, too. I almost always had the avocado on toast. When the waitress emerged from inside with our coffees, we both ordered our usual—avocado for me, and bacon and eggs for Aunt Evie.

"Is Curtis working today?" Aunt Evie asked when she'd gone.

"Yes." He joined us sometimes, which always made her happy. She thought he was the best thing since sliced bread.

"How is he doing? Is he feeling confident?"

I knew she referred to the custody hearing on Monday, and I smiled, buoyed by Paul's confidence. "You'll never believe what's happened."

I told her about catching Kelly in the act of buying drugs and the likely outcome once the judge found out. Aunt Evie actually clapped her hands.

"That's wonderful news—though you're wrong. I have absolutely no problem believing she'd do such a thing. And perhaps it's for the best, too. That woman simply isn't cut out for motherhood. Once she gets a taste of life overseas with that rich boyfriend of hers, she won't be back. Sleepy old Sunny Bay just doesn't compare. Imagine if she'd taken little Maisie with her." She shuddered theatrically. "Poor Curtis would never have seen that sweet child again."

"I don't think he could have borne it. He loves that kid." For that matter, *I* loved that kid—and I hadn't even known her a year. She was an easy person to love. Much like her father.

Aunt Evie gave me an arch look over her coffee cup. "So now Maisie will be looking for a mother figure in her life. Are you interested in taking the position?"

Certainly, no one would ever complain that Aunt Evie wasn't direct.

"We've only been going out for six months," I said mildly.

Aunt Evie made a disparaging noise. "Six *weeks* is long enough for some people to make up their mind." She gave me a playful smile. "But tell me you haven't thought about it and I won't say another word."

"I haven't thought about it," I said immediately.

She laughed. "I should have said, tell me *truthfully* that you haven't thought about it."

"Well, if we're talking about lies," I grumbled, "what about the woman who's promising to be quiet about something I know perfectly well she won't let go of?"

She reached over and patted my hand, not offended in the least. "It's been such a joy to me to see you so happy these last six months." The warmth in her smile showed her love for me, and I felt the sudden sting of moisture in my eyes. "You won't find a better man than Curtis anywhere."

I looked down at my plate to hide the tears. "You won't get any argument from me on that."

She patted my hand again, then drew back as the waitress arrived with our meals. I was grateful for the interruption. The conversation had gone in a surprisingly emotional direction. I'd been so focused on the custody hearing and making it through without losing Maisie that

I hadn't spared a thought for what might come after. What our lives might look like without the spectre of Kelly hovering like the wicked fairy at the christening, about to ruin everything. Could there be a happily ever after waiting for us on the other side?

Once the waitress had gone again, Aunt Evie picked up right where she'd left off. "You can't blame an old woman for wanting to see her beloved niece settled before she dies."

I rolled my eyes so hard it was a wonder they didn't roll right out of my head. Honestly, this woman was shameless. I smiled down at my plate and cut a neat square of avocado on toast, imagining her outrage if anyone else were to call her old. "Yes, because clearly, you're on your death bed."

"Well, I could be." She shovelled a sizeable hunk of bacon into her mouth, proving that her appetite, at least, was healthy. Once she'd chewed it, she added, "Nothing is sure in this world apart from death and taxes. And speaking of death—where are you at with your investigation?"

Grateful for a change in topic, I filled her in on the latest developments, including my chat with Justin on the beach. She listened attentively, sneaking the occasional piece of bacon to Rufus, who lurked so close to her under the table that his whiskers brushed her knee. Rufus was not a fan of avocado, and his loyalty could be bought.

"So, you think McGovern's got the right man?" she asked when I was finished.

"Most likely. I wish I could be sure, though. I still feel as if Yumi could have done it."

"What about the other brother? Aaron?"

"Angus," I corrected. "If we assume that being the CEO of Klein's World of Kristmas is worth killing for, then he has just as much motive as Travis and Yumi."

"I suppose so." Aunt Evie sounded reluctant to agree. "If you squint a bit and look at it sideways."

"Well, I grant you it's a roundabout way of getting there. It would have been simpler to just kill Travis, but perhaps he has *some* family feeling. Maybe killing Krystal and framing Travis for it felt easier than offing his own brother."

"But did he have the chance to kill Krystal? He came down from the restaurant with you and the others, so I assumed he was with them. When would he have managed it?"

"That's a good question, and I wish I had an answer for you. He wasn't actually there when I walked into the restaurant. He followed me in a few moments later. Supposedly, he'd been back to his room to grab a cardigan for his wife."

"But he might have had time to kill Krystal as well?"

I nodded. "He might have. Especially if his room is on the same floor as Travis's. I'll have to find out." It would be ironic if I'd spent all this time thinking the killer must be Travis or Yumi and it turned out to be the chronically overlooked older brother. "Stephanie told me he'd only been gone 'a few minutes', so perhaps Krystal was already dead when he went on his errand, but who knows?"

Aunt Evie took a thoughtful sip of her coffee. "*A few minutes* is annoyingly vague. And pounds to pennies his room *will* turn out to be on the third floor, so the cameras there will tell us nothing. Perhaps the cameras in the elevators could pin down the timing?"

"I'm sure they could." I sat back and gave her a frustrated shrug. "But no one will give *us* that information. We'll just have to put our faith in Detective McGovern."

Aunt Evie pulled a face that left no doubt what she thought of that idea. "Let's move on. Remind me who else was missing when you went up to the restaurant?"

"Travis, Yumi, and their son Brandon. And Krystal and Justin, of course."

"Hmm. I don't suppose the kid could have done it?"

I shook my head. "Nope. Heidi saw him in town right after the murder. He couldn't have gotten there in time."

She chewed a piece of bacon with a contemplative air. "So, it's most likely Travis or Yumi if the motive was the affair itself, or Travis or Angus if it was over the promotion."

"Don't rule out Yumi if the promotion was the motive. I wouldn't want to get on Yumi's bad side. If Krystal threatened that promotion, I could see her taking matters into her own hands. Combined with the fact that this woman was having an affair with her husband, her motive is even stronger."

Aunt Evie slipped another piece of bacon under the table. Satisfied crunching sounds could be heard. "It's always love or money, isn't it? People are basic creatures."

I thought back over the three murder cases I'd been

involved with previously, and I couldn't argue with her summary. Love—and money—made the world go round. Put them both together and you had a combination worth killing for.

CHAPTER 23

"Look, there's one of the murder people." Aunt Evie gestured at something over my shoulder.

I turned and saw Donal heading inside. He had a list and seemed to be ordering a large number of coffees to go.

"You can't call them murder people," I said. "It makes them sound like a bunch of killers. He's the nephew." So, I guessed that made him the cousin of a murderer.

"He looks like a nice boy," Aunt Evie said. Donal was probably in his mid-forties, but every man under sixty was a boy to Aunt Evie.

"He is." I finished my avocado toast and pushed the plate away with a contented sigh. "He seems very fond of his aunt. He's an accountant."

"Well, I suppose everyone has their flaws."

I snorted, but said nothing, as Donal had finished ordering and was coming our way.

"Hello, ladies." He smiled at us both, then nodded at me. "You were right—this place makes the best coffee in

town. Better than that bitter stuff they serve at the hotel."
He gave a theatrical shudder.

"Stephanie not with you this morning?" I asked.

"No. She couldn't leave Auntie Susan, so I offered to do
a coffee run. I needed to get out."

"Is something wrong with your aunt?" Aunt Evie
asked, a look of polite concern on her face.

His expression sobered. "I guess you haven't heard.
The police charged Travis this morning."

"Oh, dear." Aunt Evie's hand went to her throat in a
gesture of shock, as if we hadn't just been discussing this
very possibility.

"Did they find more evidence?" I asked. I couldn't even
decide if the killer was Travis or Yumi. Unless the police
knew more than I did, I couldn't see how they had enough
to pin it on Travis yet. I was ninety per cent sure they were
right, but still—ninety per cent wasn't the same as being
certain. Everything pointed to him, but only in a circumstantial way.

"There was a piece of glass on the balcony of Travis
and Yumi's room." I glanced at Aunt Evie, remembering
when I'd seen that piece of glass, but she was watching
Donal with rapt attention. "It had Krystal's fingerprint on
it, but when the police questioned him about what Krystal
was doing in his room, he said she hadn't been in there."

"That seems like shooting himself in the foot if they
already had fingerprint evidence," Aunt Evie said.

Donal nodded. "Right. They put it to him that she'd
been drinking there with him, and they had an argument.
She dropped the glass when he threw her over the edge.

But he kept insisting that he'd never been in the room with her, and someone must have planted it there." He gave a hollow laugh. "The police weren't buying it."

"Your poor family," I said. "Are you okay?"

"As okay as anyone can be under the circumstances. No one likes to think that their cousin is capable of such violence. I've known him since he was born." He shook his head slowly. "I can still hardly believe it. I really thought they'd find it was a robbery gone wrong or something. Someone outside the family. Now Uncle Rob's ranting, Auntie Susan is terrified he's going to have a heart attack, and Yumi won't talk to any of us. The whole family's in an uproar."

"I can see why you volunteered for the coffee run."

"Yeah. Uncle Rob's spent all morning on the phone to his lawyers."

The barista called him inside then, and he went in to pick up his order. He hesitated at the counter, and I could see immediately that he had a problem. The barista had put the coffees into little cardboard trays to make carrying them easier, but it seemed the café had run out of the trays that held four coffees, and only had the two-cup kind left. With eight coffees in four trays, Donal was short of hands.

I wiped my mouth with my serviette and stood up. "I'll give Donal a hand," I said to Aunt Evie. "Thanks for breakfast."

She flashed me a brilliant smile. "Always a pleasure, darling. Same time next week?"

"It's a date."

Rufus got up, hovering unhappily as I went inside to pay.

"Need help?" I asked Donal.

He shot me a grateful smile and stopped trying to balance two of the trays along his arm. "Would you mind? I'm afraid I didn't think this through."

"I'm so sorry, sir," the barista said, repeating what he'd clearly said before. "Normally we have the larger trays, but we're out today."

"Not a problem," I said cheerily. I held up my credit card and he rang up what we owed for breakfast. Once that was sorted, I picked up two of the trays and smiled at Donal. "Shall we? I hope you don't mind dogs."

"Love them," he said as Rufus joined us. "Hey there, boy."

Rufus wagged but quickly established that Donal had no bacon for him. Coffee was far less interesting, so he trotted off ahead of us. I had to call him back when he headed for the sand.

"We're not going home yet," I told him. He gave the seagulls a wistful look, but there were plenty of good smells to be sniffed wherever we went, so he didn't mind too much. As long as we were outside, he was happy.

"This is very kind of you," Donal said once we'd gained the path that ran along above the beach.

"Happy to help," I said. "So, your uncle is getting Travis a lawyer?"

"Yeah. This is going to get expensive fast."

"But Travis will pay, won't he?"

He snorted. "Travis and Yumi don't have two cents to rub together."

"Oh." I took a minute to digest that. "I thought—"

"You thought he was loaded? Yeah, so do most people. He likes to give that impression. Lives as though he had a money tree growing in his front yard, but it's all on credit. He's got half a dozen cards, and they're all maxed out."

"Really?" People were endlessly surprising. "I would have thought he was making good money."

Donal gave me a pitying look. "It's a family company, not a multinational. None of us are getting what you might call a competitive salary. All the non-family employees are on minimum wage, and the rest of us aren't making much more. Uncle Rob has always had a tight hold on the purse strings."

I frowned. "But you're having a conference at an expensive hotel ... and getting staff photos taken ..."

He shrugged. "Tax write-offs. Uncle Rob always gets value for money. It's a shame Travis didn't inherit some of that stinginess. I love my cousin, but he wouldn't know a budget if it hit him over the head."

Curiouser and curiouser. "He seems an odd choice to put in charge of the company, then."

"Ha! You'd think so, wouldn't you? I argued for Angus, but Travis has always been the golden boy, and Uncle Rob will hear nothing against him."

"Is Angus a better financial manager?"

He grinned at me. "Angus probably still has the first dollar he ever earned. They might be brothers, but they couldn't be more different." He puffed a little as we started the climb up the hill toward the Metropole. "Tensions have been running high around the office lately, with both of them angling for the job."

"Is it just the prestige, then?" I asked. "If the money's not great, why did they both want it?"

Donal laughed. "Oh, the money's great for *that* role. Uncle Rob never pinched pennies when it came to his own remuneration, and he could hardly pay his replacement less. Travis would have doubled his salary with that promotion. He would have done anything to get the job." He shook his head. "I just never realised he'd kill for it."

Did Detective McGovern know all this? It certainly made the case against Travis more compelling.

"But how is Krystal's death connected to all this?"

He shrugged. "She must have threatened to expose their affair. Uncle Rob would never have given the job to an adulterer. He's a bit of a puritan like that. *Family values* is practically his motto."

I nodded. I barely knew the man, but I'd already picked up on that. We turned at the Metropole and started up the long driveway toward the grand old hotel, Rufus trotting along ahead of us with his tail held at a jaunty angle.

"If there's any good to come out of this whole mess," Donal puffed, "it's that Angus will take the role now instead of his brother. Travis would probably have run the company into the ground within a year."

CHAPTER 24

My eyes went straight to the spot on the driveway where Krystal had fallen. I didn't mean to be ghoulish; I just couldn't help it. Someone had cleaned the concrete so there was no sign left that anything had happened there, but in my mind's eye, I still saw her crumpled body.

Donal nudged the door open with his butt, and I told Rufus very sternly to sit, then followed Donal inside. He pressed the button for the lift with his elbow and smiled at me, but we waited in silence. I was still thinking about Krystal and what kind of person she had been.

She'd been having an affair, which was a bit of a black mark against her character, but sometimes love made us do stupid things, and she had at least asked her husband for a divorce. Though perhaps she'd been pushed into that once he'd discovered the affair.

But it did show that she really loved Travis and wanted to be with him, which didn't sit well with my working theory that she had somehow threatened his promotion. Why would she have threatened to expose the affair? She must have known his promotion hinged on keeping up the façade of the good family man. Why would she choose this moment to try to ruin the prospects of the man she loved?

For money? But she must have known he had none, and getting the job was his only way of getting more. You'd think she'd wait until he was firmly in place in the role before putting the screws on him for money, if that was what she was doing.

The lift arrived, and we stepped in, Donal again doing his awkward shuffle so he could press the button for the fourth floor with his elbow. Maybe the lovers really had had an argument, and the murder was a spur-of-the-moment crime of passion. Maybe Travis had refused to leave Yumi and broken it off, and she'd threatened to expose him out of sheer rage, considering she'd just blown up her own marriage for him.

Donal led the way down the corridor to the suite at the end. He didn't bother knocking, just called out. Stephanie opened the door and immediately relieved him of one of his trays.

"Hi, Charlie." She gave a rueful grin when she saw me burdened with coffees. "I guess I should have gone with Donal after all. Sorry to drag you all the way up here."

"It's no problem," I said, helping her hand out coffees. The barista had marked the tops of all of them, so it was easy to tell which was which. "Cappuccino?"

"That's me," Mr Klein said, accepting the drink with a distracted smile. He was in the middle of typing out a text, using one finger in the hunt-and-peck method so common to people of his generation.

"I'm sorry to hear about Travis," I said.

He looked up at that, his finger hovering over his screen. "I can't believe that fool of a detective is wasting time persecuting Travis when he should be out hunting for the real killer. He'll be sorry when my lawyers have finished with him."

Behind his back, Stephanie rolled her eyes, but no one argued with him.

"I just don't understand why *anyone* would want to kill poor Krystal," Mrs Klein said. She was holding a coffee but hadn't drunk from it. The poor woman looked as though she hadn't had a good night's sleep all week.

"Exactly," her husband said. "Nobody would. It must have been a burglar."

Mrs Klein only looked more confused. "But why was she in Travis's room at all? It doesn't make sense."

Half the people in the room looked at Yumi, while the other half tried very hard *not* to. By now, all of them knew about the affair. The answer did seem obvious, but perhaps not to the golden boy's mother.

Mr Klein shook his head emphatically. "My son isn't a murderer."

Stephanie sighed. "You didn't think he was an adulterer, either, but here we are."

Yumi shot an anxious glance at her son, then gave Stephanie a filthy look. She needn't have worried; Brandon had accepted a coffee without even looking up from whatever game he was playing on his phone.

"Come on, Dad, seriously?" Angus asked. "A burglar? Give me a break. We all know it was either him or Yumi, don't we? The rest of us were together in the restaurant."

Interesting. Was Angus emphasising "us" all being together in the restaurant, hoping everyone would forget he'd ducked out at the crucial time to get his wife's cardigan?

Yumi jumped in before I could open my mouth. "How do we know it wasn't *you*? You *said* you were going back to your room, but maybe you took a little detour."

"Why would *I* kill Krystal?" he scoffed. "*I* wasn't the one having an affair with her. And very conveniently, *you* were supposedly in Brandon's room, where nobody saw you. And Travis supposedly was in *his*, yet somehow, magically, he's somewhere else when the murder takes place."

"He said he went out for a smoke," Yumi said, lifting her chin. "And I believe him."

"Funny how he only comes up with that story when he gets accused of murder. Before that, we have Brandon here making up lies about how they went off to buy ice cream together, as if anyone would believe that." He snorted. "Yeah, father-son bonding. That sounds like Travis."

I felt as confused as Mrs Klein. "Why didn't he just *say* he was smoking? Why lie over a cigarette?"

"Because he was supposed to have given up," Stephanie said. "And he was too much of a coward to come clean in front of his wife."

"Stop it, both of you," Mr Klein snapped. "This is your

brother you're talking about. Are you saying you think he did it? How could you? Where's your loyalty?"

"Just because he's my brother doesn't mean he has no flaws," Angus said. "Although of course you and Mum refuse to see them."

"He *was* about to go bankrupt," Donal said mildly.

"That's not true!" Yumi hissed.

Brandon was staring fixedly at his phone, head down and shoulders hunched, probably wishing he were anywhere but here while the adults fought all around him. I was starting to feel the same, and took a step toward the door, ready to make my apologies and leave.

"What does it matter?" Mr Klein roared. "Who cares if he didn't have two cents to rub together? Killing Krystal doesn't magically make him rich!"

"But getting the CEO position would," Angus said into the heavy silence. "Funny how *your* role is the only one that gets a decent salary in this company."

Father and son glared at each other. Both their faces were red and wore matching expressions that suggested a refusal to back down. I took another step toward the door.

Mr Klein cast around for an outlet for his fury, and his eye fell on Brandon. "Is that boy still on his phone? No wonder his generation have no conversational skills— they're all permanently attached to their stupid phones. Put that thing away, boy, and talk to your family."

Yumi turned on him. "Maybe he'd want to talk to you if you made even the tiniest effort. But no. You go on and on about the importance of family, but you're the worst grandfather in the world. The only time you talk to

Brandon is when you're complaining about something. You don't like his haircut. You don't like his clothes. Nothing he does is ever good enough for you." Mr Klein started to sputter, but she wasn't done. "All this talk about family is just that—talk. This family is so fractured." Her angry gaze raked them all in turn. "Angus hates Travis, Stephanie resents them both. Susan just sits there and lets you stomp all over everyone in your big boots like the petty dictator you are, thinking you're so great because you founded this stupid company. It's just Christmas decorations, Robert. You're not curing cancer."

Everyone stared, shocked into silence by her outburst. If Mr Klein's face got any redder, we'd be calling an ambulance. The last thing we needed now was a heart attack.

"How dare you speak to me like that?" he snarled at her.

"It's about time someone did," she said, refusing to be cowed. Even Brandon had looked up from his phone, staring at his mother in surprise. "It's not phones that ruin relationships, it's people. You might want to think about that." She stood up. "Come on, Brandon. We don't have to put up with this."

Brandon didn't have to be told twice. He leapt off the couch as if he'd been launched from a cannon.

His mother surveyed the room, her lip curled with disgust. "I can't believe you people are all squabbling like this while Travis is in *jail*."

Angus gave her a scornful look. "Are you sure you've got your key this time? They say third time's the charm."

Nervous laughter broke the tension in the room,

though Donal looked as confused as me. "What?" he asked.

"She's lost it twice before," Stephanie said, clearly happy to be talking about something less explosive. "You remember what a fuss she made at dinner the night of the murder." When his expression didn't change, she added, "When she couldn't find it? That was why Travis initially decided to go with her, and then he said he had calls to make anyway, remember?"

"Oh, that must have been when he was in the bathroom," Delphine said.

I stopped, my feet suddenly rooted to the floor. Donal had been to the bathroom? I stared at his affable face, my brain clicking into overdrive. The small round bruise on his chin had faded to a pale green now, barely noticeable.

"Remember," Delphine added helpfully, "he came back in as they were leaving?"

"When was that?" The urgency in my tone brought Donal's gaze to my face. "How long before I came in to tell you Krystal was dead?"

Stephanie was the first to catch on. "Only about ten minutes," she said slowly. "Maybe even five."

"More like half an hour," Donal said with an easy laugh. "You'd had too many wines to keep track of the time."

"No, I don't think it was." She was still staring at him, a thoughtful gleam in her eye. "You know, you were gone quite a long time."

Comprehension dawned on Angus's face, too. "That's right. I was thinking I'd have to go make sure you were all right, then you finally came back. Just before I went to get Del's cardigan."

My heart pounded as they both stared at him speculatively. Donal? *Really?* I could hear Aunt Evie in my head saying he seemed like a nice boy. But that bruise was an odd shape to be caused by walking into a door in the middle of the night, as he'd claimed. On reflection, it seemed far more like the kind of bruise that you'd get from being accidentally struck in the face by a stiletto heel as you pushed its wearer off a balcony.

What if I had the timeline all wrong? Everyone was so vague about *when* things had happened—and I'd known from the beginning that a few minutes either way could be the difference between innocent and guilty.

I'd assumed all along that Travis and Yumi had left the dinner before Krystal died, making one of them the most likely killer. But what if they'd actually left *after* she was already dead? None of them were sure of the timings of their comings and goings. If they truly hadn't left the restaurant until five minutes before I appeared to tell them Krystal was dead, then they were in the clear.

And the person who'd been returning to the restaurant as they left, after an unusually long absence ... suddenly *that* person looked horribly guilty.

"I'm sure no one wants to hear about my toilet habits," Donal said. He forced a smile, but his posture was tense. The genial companion who'd chatted to me on the way up from the beach was gone. He'd seemed so friendly, yet all that seemingly artless chatter had implicated Travis even further. But in the middle of all that finger-pointing, he'd mentioned that the non-family staff were on minimum wage.

So, Krystal had no money for expensive jewellery. Neither did her lover, though perhaps he was putting it on credit—Donal had been keen to tell me about Travis's maxed-out credit cards, because it made it look like he had a motive. Perhaps Krystal was stealing from the company that refused to pay her what she was worth.

Although you'd think the accountant would have noticed that.

"Mr Klein," I said, "why do you pay your staff so poorly?"

All eyes turned to me. I admit, it looked like a non sequitur. Stephanie and her brother were halfway to accusing Donal of murder; no doubt it seemed a bad moment for a detour into company policy.

Mr Klein reddened even further. "That's none of your business."

"I think it might be relevant to your son's predicament," I said. "Is the business doing badly? Is that why you can't afford to pay more?"

"There's not a lot of money in Christmas decorations," Donal said tightly. If looks could kill, I'd be writhing on the floor right now. Clearly, he didn't think this line of questioning was much of an improvement on the previous one. Funny about that.

Mr Klein sighed. "No, not like there used to be."

"Has there been a downturn lately? Like, since Krystal joined the company?"

He frowned, and out of the corner of my eye, I saw Donal stiffen.

"What are you suggesting, young lady?" Mr Klein demanded.

"You shouldn't speak ill of the dead," his wife protested weakly, but everyone else seemed riveted by the conversation.

Just last month, I'd read a news article about a small company that lost over a hundred thousand dollars because their receptionist was changing the bank details on the company invoices to her own bank account before she sent the invoices out. She'd gotten away with it for a long time because if anyone ever rang to check the bank account details before they paid, she was the one who took the call and confirmed that everything was correct.

My mind was racing at a million miles an hour, but I still felt as though I were missing something. Had Donal killed her because he caught her embezzling from the company? That didn't feel right. Sure, he'd be angry, but angry enough to kill? That was such an extreme reaction it really made no sense. Why not just expose her? That way, the law would be on his side, and the company might even have a chance to get back some of the funds.

Whereas if the opposite were true and *Donal* was the one embezzling, suddenly the murder made a lot more sense. If Krystal had found out and threatened to expose him, Donal risked losing not only his job and his freedom but probably his whole family. That was one steaming heap of motivation right there.

"Never mind," I said, cutting off Mr Klein's righteous outrage. "Who does the invoicing for your company?"

Stephanie and Angus looked at each other.

"Donal does, of course," their father said angrily.

I thought as much, but I had to check. There might have been some junior employee I didn't know about whose job it was. "I wonder if all your clients are actually paying you."

"Of course they are," Mr Klein said.

"Not that it's any of your business," Donal added. "I think it's time for you to go."

"What's the rush?" Stephanie sounded casual, but her face was taut with anger. "I, for one, am very interested in Charlie's theories."

I held Mr Klein's gaze. "What I mean is, are your clients paying *you* or someone else? Whose bank account details are on the invoices they receive?"

"This is ridiculous," Donal blustered. "You can look at every invoice in our system. They all have the company bank account details on the bottom. I really don't like what you're insinuating here."

Well, that made two of us. I didn't like it, either, but sadly, that didn't make me wrong. The more I thought about it, the more the puzzle pieces slotted into place.

The night of the murder, Yumi had got up to leave dinner and realised she'd lost her room key. Donal could have taken it. I'd have to find out where she'd been sitting, but there'd been an empty chair beside him when I came in to tell them Krystal was dead. Dollars to donuts it had been Yumi's chair, and Donal had filched her key while she was sitting there.

The cameras on the third floor were out. I wondered now if Donal had somehow arranged that, or if he'd just gotten lucky. Either way, I was sure he knew about it. He also must have known there were cameras in the lifts, so he wouldn't have used them to move from the restaurant to the third floor. The Metropole was an old hotel, so old that it had been built before lifts in hotels became commonplace, and there was still a grand staircase connecting all levels of the hotel.

He would have walked up those stairs and let himself into Travis and Yumi's room with his stolen key, while the others thought he was on an extended bathroom break. All he had to do then was lure Krystal to the room.

Stephanie put her hands on her hips. "Well, obviously they have Klein's bank account details on them in the *system*, Donal. No one's accusing you of being stupid, just dishonest."

"And a murderer," Angus added.

"The question is," Stephanie continued, "do the invoices in the system accurately reflect all the work that gets done? Or do some of our clients get a special invoice that *doesn't* get recorded?"

She pulled out her phone, called someone, and put it on speakerphone so we could all hear the phone ringing.

"Yeah, hi, it's Steph Klein," she said when the person on the other end answered. "Can you email me a copy of the last invoice you got from us? Yeah, right away. Sorry to bother you on the weekend, but it's urgent."

There was a little more, but I was watching Donal's face and not listening properly. He was breathing fast, and one hand was clenching and unclenching at his side. Soon, Stephanie hung up and began tapping her screen.

"I don't have to stay here and listen to this rubbish." Donal strode angrily toward the door, but Angus stepped to block his way.

"Donal," Mr Klein barked. "Sit down."

There was a frozen silence until Stephanie's phone beeped to signal an incoming email. She opened the email and studied it for a moment, her face expressionless. Then she got up and showed the phone to her dad.

"Is that our bank account?"

Mr Klein pulled out his own phone, and we were subjected to another round of squinting and one-finger pecking. Finally, he found what he was looking for.

He looked up, his face white. "No."

CHAPTER 25

DONAL LUNGED FOR THE DOOR, CATCHING ANGUS, WHO WAS still staring at his father in shock, by surprise. He grabbed Donal's shirt, but Donal whacked him across the face and broke free. It was up to Yumi, who surprised everyone by throwing herself at him in a football tackle, to bring him crashing to the floor.

I knew those powerful arms of hers would come in handy.

"You lying dog!" she yelled at him, striking at his face with her fists. Frankly, that was an insult to dogs, but I would never hurt Rufus's feelings by repeating it. Donal writhed beneath her, simultaneously trying to shield his face and throw her off, but she was sitting on top of him and would not be budged. "My husband's in jail right now because of you. You killed her, didn't you!" She punctuated that with another whack to the head before Angus caught her arm and dragged her away.

"Yes, thank you, Yumi, that'll do," he said, though I

noticed he'd let Yumi get in a few good hits before he'd stopped her. His right cheek was bright red where Donal had struck him.

Yumi stood, breathing heavily, and smoothed down the sleek cream fabric of her skirt. Donal staggered to his feet, and Angus shoved him roughly toward a chair. Everyone else found their seats again, and I perched uncomfortably on the edge of a lounge next to Stephanie, watching Yumi glare daggers at Donal. A lot of very good coffee was going to waste, abandoned on side tables as everyone stared at Donal with varying degrees of shock and horror.

"Well," Mr Klein said at last, "I suppose someone had better call the police."

"I'll do it," Stephane said, pulling out her phone again. We all listened as she gave Detective McGovern a very brief rundown of what had just happened, then hung up and looked at her father. "He's on his way."

I would definitely have to be gone before he got here, which didn't give me much time, considering the police station was only ten minutes away. What were my chances of persuading the others not to mention that I'd even been here at all?

Reluctantly, I decided it was probably best not to ask them to start lying to the police. That was a bad habit to get into—though goodness knows enough of them had already been indulging in it. I didn't envy Detective McGovern the job that awaited him in getting it all straightened out.

Poor Mr Klein looked absolutely shellshocked, and my

heart went out to him. I knew he was in his early seventies, but he'd never really struck me as *old* until the moment I saw the devastation on his face.

He drew himself up in his chair, fortifying himself by reaching for his wife's hand. His lined face was pale, the angry red all drained away. "Do you have anything to say for yourself before the detective arrives? You killed poor Krystal, and you've stolen from your own family. How *could* you, Donal? I trusted you."

Donal gave an ugly laugh. "Funny, for someone who blathers on so much about the importance of family, you're a real miser when it comes to paying them. You seem to expect us all to work for you for peanuts, just because we're *family*."

Stephanie's voice was hard. "So, you gave yourself an unofficial pay rise, did you?"

Donal shrugged. "It was easy enough. The accounting system hasn't been updated since the Stone Age." He cast a scornful glance at his uncle. "That would cost money, wouldn't it? So, I scrubbed a few invoices from the system and sent out my own invoices for the work."

"With your bank account in place of the company's," Angus said, his eyes flat, his words clipped with anger.

"That's right."

"So, the clients thought they were paying us what they owed." Stephanie shook her head. "No wonder we never seemed to make a profit."

Mrs Klein waved her free hand. The other was still firmly clutched in her husband's. "Never mind all that.

What about Krystal?" A pleading note entered her voice. "Tell me you didn't really kill her."

Donal looked down at his hands, abashed for seemingly the first time, but he didn't say anything. I remembered how gently he'd treated Mrs Klein on the night of the murder. Now he couldn't even look at her. Was that a faint stirring of guilt as his reputation in the eyes of his aunt was forever destroyed?

"But why?" poor Mrs Klein persisted, her voice plaintive, as if she were begging Donal to help her understand. "What did she ever do to you?"

"You'd be surprised." The words burst from him like water from a dam. "Krystal was no angel. She discovered what I was doing, and instead of reporting me like a good girl, she blackmailed me instead. I paid her five grand a month to keep quiet."

"Five grand a *month*?" Angus repeated in tones of disbelief.

"How much were *you* making?" Stephanie asked.

If he could afford to give away five grand to buy Krystal's silence, it must have been considerably more.

Donal shook his head. "You don't want to know. She came to me last month and said the price had gone up. Now she wanted ten grand a month to keep her mouth shut. I could see how it would be—I was totally at her mercy. She'd keep upping the price of her silence until I'd have to take so much that either someone would twig to what was going on or the company would go bust. Something had to be done."

Good heavens, the finality in that last sentence. He

sounded so clinical, when he was talking about a woman's life.

"So, you killed her," Stephanie said. It wasn't a question.

"Yes." Now that he'd started talking, it was if he couldn't stop until everyone knew how clever he'd been. "When Krystal and Justin left dinner early that night, it seemed like a golden opportunity. I took Yumi's room key from her bag."

"You were sitting next to me," Yumi said.

He nodded. "Your bag was right there at my feet. Then I said I was going to the bathroom and went downstairs to your room instead."

She regarded him as if he were some kind of insect she'd like to step on. "And you told Krystal you had to talk? Didn't she find it odd that you were in our room?"

"No." He looked pleased with himself. "Travis's phone was charging in your room." He glanced at me. "Uncle Rob hates people bringing their phones to dinner. Ruins his *family conversation* if everyone's on their phones. I used it to send a text to her private phone, pretending to be Travis." He smiled at Yumi, and it wasn't a pleasant smile. "I knew all about the affair and the secret phone she kept. She came over straight away, of course, thinking Travis had snuck away from dinner for a bit of slap and tickle. I think she'd been expecting the message."

Yumi flinched at this description, and Stephanie gave him a disgusted look.

"She laughed when she arrived and it was me instead." His expression darkened. "She was so sure she had the upper hand. She poured herself a drink from the minibar and went out to the balcony. Thought she was going to put me in my place. So, I told her the gravy train was over. She wasn't getting another cent out of me."

The room had gone silent, everyone spellbound by his recount. I could picture Krystal on the balcony in her pretty red dress, full of self-confidence, glass of wine in hand. It must never have crossed her mind that she was in danger. Donal's mild-mannered accountant façade had fooled her the way it had fooled me.

"She didn't like that, did she?" A cruel smile touched his lips. "She thought she could dictate terms, but she had no power. Didn't look so full of herself when I grabbed her legs and tipped her over the edge." His smile widened, and a shiver ran through me. How could anyone recall killing another human being with such fondness?

"And the wine glass broke?" I prompted him.

"Yes. I cleaned it up quickly. Must have missed a piece in the dark." That was the piece I'd noticed when Aunt Evie and I were searching Travis's room—the one Detective McGovern had found Krystal's fingerprint on. "One of her shoes fell off, too. I dropped that in my room on the way back to the restaurant and dumped it the next day. The whole thing took less than ten minutes. I was back in time to wish Yumi and Travis goodnight."

Tears swam in Mrs Klein's eyes. "You're a monster. All this over money."

"I didn't become an accountant for the joy of numbers," he sneered. "Money makes the world go around, and I wanted my share."

"You could have worked for it like an honest man," Angus said, disgust on his face.

The doorbell rang, and I jumped. I'd been so caught up in the story that I'd forgotten all about Detective McGovern. Now my heart sank as Stephanie opened the door to him and he stepped into the room.

He scowled when he caught sight of me. "What are *you* doing here?"

I leapt to my feet. "Just leaving! Excuse me, everyone. I'll leave you to talk to the detective."

I slipped past him and out into the corridor. Before the door fell shut, I heard Mr Klein launching into an explanation of how "that young lady just uncovered the real killer when you idiots put my son into jail". I cringed as I hurried down the hall.

Detective McGovern wouldn't be joining my fan club any time soon.

CHAPTER 26

MONDAY AFTERNOON PASSED AS IF EVERY MINUTE WERE AN HOUR. Time oozed by at the speed of molasses. I was supposed to be editing some headshots for a client—I had quite a backlog of work, now, due to the distraction of the murder case—but my focus was completely gone. Every few minutes, I checked my phone, certain that I somehow must have missed a call despite hovering over that phone like a mother hen over her eggs.

All my willing the phone to ring with an update from Sydney was in vain, though, and it remained stubbornly silent. Surely, the custody hearing was over by now? It was almost four o'clock.

Maybe they'd started late. These things were often delayed. Maybe it had run longer than anyone expected. That possibility made me distinctly nervous, because, surely, our case against Kelly was pretty open and shut. It should have been over quickly. The fact that Curtis hadn't called me yet to tell me what had happened left a sinking feeling in the pit of my stomach.

I refused to accept that anything could have gone wrong. But if we'd won, why hadn't he rung with the good news? Once again, I wished he'd accepted my offer to go with him as moral support, but he'd said it was something he needed to handle on his own, so I'd respected his wishes.

Stupid wishes. The suspense was *killing* me.

Rufus sighed heavily as I got up to pace once again.

"Oh, I'm sorry," I said with heavy sarcasm. "Am I disturbing your beauty sleep?"

His eyebrows twitched, but that was the only attention he paid me. Maybe I should get out and take him for a walk. It would do us both good, and it wasn't as though I was getting much work done.

I picked up my phone for the thousandth time to check my texts. My last hopeful text to Curtis—*Any news?*—was still sitting there, unanswered. I let out a sigh to rival Rufus's and dropped the phone back on the table. There was no point ringing him. If he was still in the hearing, he wouldn't be able to answer anyway.

The doorbell rang. Rufus and I both perked up. I wasn't expecting any deliveries, but maybe it was Jack. Monday night was often our pizza night, if he wasn't working. Perhaps he wanted to say something about that. I hurried to the door, happy for any kind of distraction.

I barely had it open before Curtis swept me into his arms. "We did it! I have sole custody." He whispered the words against my cheek as he crushed me against him. "It's all thanks to you."

My eyes filled with happy tears as I returned the hug with enthusiasm. "Sole custody? Seriously? That's wonderful news." They had shared custody before. Even with Kelly moving overseas, we'd expected the judge to continue that arrangement.

"The judge said he wouldn't trust her to look after a dog," Curtis murmured in my ear.

Wow. That was some plain speaking. Kelly really had shot herself in the foot. She'd tried to take everything and ended up with nothing.

A piping voice interrupted, sounding a little indignant. "It's my turn to hug Charlie now, Daddy."

We broke apart, and I beamed down at Maisie. "I'm always ready for a hug. I think Rufus might like one, too." He was wagging like a maniac, trying to insert himself between Curtis and me, the whole back half of his body wiggling.

"You have to wait your turn," Maisie told Rufus as I scooped her up for a hug. She wound her arms around my neck so fiercely I might have choked to death if I wasn't familiar with her hugging style already. "Daddy said Mummy will still come and visit me lots even though she won't live in Australia anymore. She will, won't she?"

Her face was pressed into my neck, and her voice sounded a little shaky. I wouldn't be surprised if Kelly disappeared into a luxury lifestyle in Europe and almost forgot she had a daughter, but I would never tell Maisie that. At the same time, I didn't want to give her false hope.

I bit my lip and exchanged a glance with Curtis, who grimaced.

"You know," I said carefully, "there are all sorts of ways to keep in touch on the computer now, or even on the phone, where you and Mummy can chat and see each other. I bet you'll hardly even notice she's gone."

"I suppose so," she muttered into my neck.

I led the way inside, Maisie still in my arms. Her legs hung down to my knees. She was getting too big for me to lift as easily as I used to even last year.

"Have you had another growth spurt?" I asked in a voice of deep suspicion, hoping to distract her. "I'm sure you weren't this big last week."

She lifted her head at last and giggled, an infectious bubbling sound. "Don't be silly, Charlie."

I dropped her on the lounge, and she squealed happily as she bounced among the cushions. Rufus barked and leapt up beside her, eager to join the fun. She threw her arms around his neck, and he licked her cheek with great gusto.

"He kissed me!"

"That's because he's excited to see you." I smiled at Curtis. He looked a different man to the last time I'd seen him, the marks of worry smoothed from his face. Seeing him so happy gave me a warm glow of satisfaction. "Why didn't you call me? I thought you must have still been in the hearing, and I was starting to get worried."

A guilty expression flitted across his face before the smile returned. "We wanted to give you the news in person."

"And the ice cream, Daddy!" Maisie said sternly. "Don't forget the ice cream."

"And I promised a certain someone we could go to the ice cream shop." He gave his daughter a fond look. "I told Maisie she can have as much ice cream as she wants."

"I'm going to have every flavour in the shop," she announced.

That seemed unlikely, considering the size of her stomach and the fact that they had at least twenty flavours, but who was I to crush her dreams?

"That's … a lot of ice cream."

"I'll share it with you, if you want," she said magnanimously.

Curtis put a hand to his heart, pretending to be hurt. "What about me? Will you share it with me, too?"

"You eat too much."

Pragmatism. I loved it.

We all piled into Curtis's big four-wheel-drive, even Rufus. He was always happy to go for a ride, even if there would be no ice cream for him at the end of it. We found a parking spot, and Maisie held both our hands as we headed for the ice cream shop.

"What flavour are you going to have?" she asked me. "They're all good. Except liquorice. Liquorice is gross."

I wasn't going to argue with that, even if Heidi might. I was just glad Maisie had forgotten about Mummy's imminent departure for the moment. Kelly might be a terrible mother, but she was the only one Maisie had ever known, so it was natural for her to be upset that Kelly was moving away. Curtis promising ice cream as a distraction was a stroke of genius.

I chose a caramel swirl, then persuaded Maisie to start with only three choices, just in case she got full. "You can order more afterwards if you have room," I suggested.

She eyed the brightly coloured tubs of ice cream wistfully, but eventually decided on choc chip, peppermint, and bubble gum, which was such a neon pink it almost hurt my eyes to look at it.

While Maisie was still checking out the merchandise, Heidi came into the shop.

"Hi!" I gave her a quick hug. "I was just thinking about you. Aren't you working today?"

"I am." She looked a little guilty. "But the shop was quiet, and I had such a craving for ice cream that I had to duck out to get some."

"What's with all the ice cream cravings lately?" I asked, thinking of how she'd alibied Justin and Brandon on the night of the murder because she'd stopped for ice cream on the way home from drinks. I meant it as a joke, but she got an odd look on her face. An almost furtive look.

I eyed the blush colouring her cheeks and suspicion took root in my mind. She'd seemed kind of off lately, and now the cravings ...

"Do you have something to tell me?"

She cast a wild look around the shop, though Curtis and Maisie were the only other people in here, and they were both occupied for the moment with Maisie's order. "I wasn't going to say anything for another couple of weeks."

Her hand crept to her stomach, and my suspicions crystallised into certainty.

"You're pregnant," I breathed, a thrill of excitement running through me.

She gave a sheepish smile. "Yeah. A bit."

"How many weeks are you?"

"Ten. The baby's due in February."

"Weren't Zach and Noah born in February?"

"Yeah. I don't know how they'll feel about getting a little brother or sister for a birthday present."

"That's so exciting," I said, giving her another hug. "Congratulations! How have you been feeling?"

"Awful." She pulled a face. "Throwing up my breakfast most days, still feeling dodgy at lunchtime—and then hit with massive cravings for ice cream in the afternoon. I feel like I'm going crazy."

"Were you like that with the twins?"

"Worse. But I started to feel better once I hit the second trimester, so hopefully I only have to put up with this for a couple more weeks. In the meantime ... hello, rum and raisin ice cream."

I frowned. "Is that safe?"

She laughed. "Don't worry. No actual rum was harmed in the making of it. It's just flavouring." She stepped up to the counter, smiling at Curtis and Maisie, and placed her order.

Maisie showed me her cardboard bowl with its three scoops of ice cream. "Do you want to try mine?"

"No thanks." I took my cone from Curtis and offered it

to her. I knew her offer actually meant *she* wanted to try *mine*. "Want to try this one?"

She took a big chunk of it, leaving caramel swirled across half her face, then we settled at one of the plastic tables outside. Heidi said goodbye as she headed back to work, and we tucked into our ice cream in contented silence, soaking up the winter sunshine.

"I've taken the rest of the week off work," Curtis said eventually. "I need to get a few things organised."

"Like what?"

"Before and after school care for Maisie on the days I'm working. Mum's offered to take her when I have night shifts."

"I can help too," I said.

He turned the full force of his smile on me. "That's really kind of you, but you have your own life. I need to make sure I can manage this on my own."

"They say it takes a village," I reminded him. "I really wouldn't mind."

I supposed I should be grateful that he hadn't just assumed I'd be available, but I felt a sting of disappointment instead. We were a team, weren't we? Maybe it was too soon. He was so used to being let down by Kelly, and fiercely determined to be both mother and father to his little girl to make up for her lack. He hadn't even let me go to the custody hearing to support him, for heaven's sake. He was aggressively independent. I wished he realised I wasn't going to leave him in the lurch.

I'd just have to prove to him that I was the kind of girl who stuck around.

To no one's surprise but her own, Maisie couldn't finish her ice cream. Curtis made the noble sacrifice of finishing for her, then offered the empty bowl to Rufus, who licked the remnants off the sides with great attention to detail.

"Are you coming to Jack's tonight for pizza?" I asked when we got back to my place.

He looked over his shoulder at Maisie in the back seat patting Rufus. "It's been a big day. I think we'd better have an early night instead."

"I'm not tired, Daddy," Maisie insisted, though she sank her own case by yawning and closing her eyes.

"There's always next week," he told her. We smiled at each other, both aware that now there was an endless vista of Monday nights together with Maisie—and every other night, too. It had been a long time coming. I could tell from his smile how excited he was to become a full-time parent again. He leaned over and kissed me softly. "It was my lucky day when you decided to move to Sunny Bay. Thank you, Charlie."

"For moving?"

He checked Maisie again before he answered. She was already asleep. "For being your wonderful, curious self. Those photos clinched the deal."

I smiled at him. "Taking photos is what I do. And also being curious, though I bet Detective McGovern would have another word for it."

"Rumour around the station says he's put in for a transfer." His dimple peeked out. "I don't think he can stand having you swoop in and solve his cases all the time."

"It's not as though I *mean* to," I protested. Had I really driven the poor detective away? "Now I feel guilty."

"Don't. You saved an innocent man, caught a guilty one, and got justice for the victim and her family. That's not a small thing. You should never feel bad for being such a light in the world." He leaned over and gave me another kiss. "I'll call you tomorrow, okay?"

"Okay." I got out and extracted Rufus from the back seat, which woke Maisie, who had to deliver several last pats before I could shut the door.

As the car backed down the driveway, Maisie let down the rear window and waved. "I love you, Charlie!" she shouted with the kind of enthusiasm only a seven-year-old could muster.

"I love you, too," I called back and waved until they were out of sight. "She's such a cutie," I said to Rufus.

He wagged. I took that as agreement.

CHAPTER 27

I KNOCKED ON JACK'S FRONT DOOR A COUPLE OF HOURS LATER. When the door opened, I blinked, then did an exaggerated doubletake. "*Jack*? Is that *you*?"

"Shut up." A blush started up newly revealed cheeks. He'd shaved his beard. *And* gotten a haircut. "Are you gonna come in or stand there staring all night?"

Rufus didn't need to be asked twice. He headed straight inside, looking around eagerly for Jack's cat Sherlock, with whom he had formed an unlikely friendship.

I followed my dog, still shaking my head in wonderment at Jack's new look. The haircut had tamed his unruly curls. It was shaved super short on the sides but longer on top, allowing a hint of his natural curl without being messy. He looked *hot*. And who knew there'd been such a strong jaw under all that beard? "You look amazing."

"Thanks." He led the way through to the kitchen at the back. His duplex was the mirror image of mine: lounge room and stairs to the upper level at the front, kitchen at the back opening onto ... well, in that way, his side of the duplex was different. Mine opened onto a small paved area, but because of the slope of our block, his back door was higher off the ground than mine. Not long after he'd moved in, he'd had a big deck built outside, and that was where we usually gathered for pizza night. He paused at the fridge. "Want a drink?"

"Sure. I'll have a cider, thanks."

He grabbed two cans, and we headed out to the deck to settle into his big comfy lounges, Rufus sprawled at our feet. There was no sign of Sherlock—he'd probably decided to stay warm upstairs. It was chilly out here, and Jack tossed me one of the blankets he kept folded in a box by the door.

I gestured at him with my can. "So why the change?"

He shrugged. "I was getting a bit tired of the beard. It's a nuisance when you have to wear a mask. And then once I'd shaved it off, my hair looked messy, so I went in for a haircut on my way home from work."

"It looks great," I said. "Though you must be feeling the cold without the beard."

He rubbed his naked chin and smiled. "Yeah, I didn't think that one through. Should have shaved it off in summer when it was all hot and scratchy." He shifted, adjusting the collar of his shirt, and a wave of aftershave reached me on the cool air.

Wait a minute. A shirt with a collar—and a nice sweater over it—aftershave, and a new, trim look. I narrowed my eyes thoughtfully. "Are we expecting someone else?" I asked casually.

"Andrea said she might pop in later." Then he looked away, and I could have sworn he was blushing again. "And I asked Priya over. I figured you could tell us how the custody hearing went all at once."

Right. And that was *definitely* the only reason he'd asked Priya over.

"You know, you don't have to pretend to me that you don't fancy Priya. I am *all* in favour of you making a move on her. You should have done it months ago."

He threw his hands up. "I tried, but she brushed me off, and she's been treating me like her kid brother ever since." He shook his head. "I should never have agreed to pretend to be her boyfriend. I thought she liked me, but ever since then, she's been holding me at arm's length."

I shook my head. He would get no argument from me. I'd said all along that the fake romance was a stupid idea, and it had turned out pretty much as badly as I'd feared. The most ridiculous part was that they both liked each other, but that one dumb decision had thrown them right off track.

I eyed all his newly shorn hotness. "I think she might be more open to persuasion now."

The front doorbell rang, and he went back inside to answer it. I snuggled down into my blanket, my feet up on the lounge, and drank my cider. We'd probably end up inside again after we'd eaten—it was really getting too cold to stay outside at night—but it was peaceful on the deck. I watched a bat flit overhead, a small black shape against the dark sky, and sighed in contentment. It was so quiet here I could hear the shushing of the waves against the shore. I would never live in a big city again.

Jack returned with Andrea and Priya, who'd arrived at the same time. Sherlock followed them, much to Rufus's delight. For a few minutes, we were distracted with deciding which pizzas to order, then we settled down and everyone looked at me expectantly.

"Well?" said Priya. "How did it go?"

I knew the *it* she referred to was the custody case, so I spent a very happy few minutes filling them in. Andrea hadn't heard about the photos I'd taken of Kelly, so I had to show those around while everyone shook their heads at her monumental stupidity.

"Though it's just as well she's such an idiot," Andrea said, "otherwise she might have dragged that poor kid off to Europe with her, never to be seen again."

It was a sobering thought, but fortunately one I didn't have to spend much time on, now that the story had a happy ending.

"And speaking of idiots," Jack said, idly stroking the cat, who had curled up in his lap, "what happened with that guy who was bonking his dad's secretary? I heard the police arrested him. Did he really kill her?"

So then we had to go through everything I'd discovered. You could have heard a pin drop while I told them about that last confrontation where Stephanie, Angus, and I all realised that Donal was the killer at the same time.

"This is like something out of a movie," Andrea said, her eyes wide.

The pizza arrived then—tandoori chicken for Priya

and me, and pepperoni for Andrea and Jack—so we ate while I told them what Curtis had said about Detective McGovern applying for a transfer, and how guilty I felt.

"That's rubbish," Jack said at once. "If he can't stand the heat—"

"He should get out of the kitchen," Priya finished, and they regarded each other with approval.

I caught Andrea's eye, and we smiled at each other before returning to our pizza. Priya was sitting directly opposite Jack, and she had spent most of the evening sneaking little glances at him. The new look was as much of a hit as I'd predicted.

"It's his own fault, anyway," Priya added, once she could tear her eyes away from Jack. "He makes such a drama about warning you not to interfere every time, so then he looks stupid at the end when you show him up."

Jack nodded. "That's right. If he would stop being so proud and work with you instead of against you, it would look like a team effort."

"Technically, he's not supposed to get help from outside the police force," I pointed out.

"Technically shmechnically," Priya said dismissively. "No one's suggesting he put you on the payroll. But asking your opinion on a couple of things wouldn't kill him. Or so you'd think. Some men just can't abide asking for help."

"Well, I'm not one of them," Jack said, jumping up to clear away the pizzas. "Want to help me get dessert ready?"

Priya leapt up immediately. "Ooh, dessert! What are we having?"

I didn't hear his answer as the back door closed behind them too quickly. Sherlock, annoyed at losing his heat source, leapt down from the lounge and stalked over to where Rufus was stretched out. Rufus opened one eye and thumped his tail lazily in greeting as the cat curled up against his back and went back to sleep.

Andrea and I sat and chatted about books—what else? We were in the middle of a heated discussion about Jules Verne when she said, "Dessert is taking forever. I wonder what on earth they're doing?"

"Maybe something's gone wrong." I stood up, ready to offer assistance. "Jack likes trying new recipes, but he doesn't always follow them properly. There could be eggs all over the kitchen. I'll go and see if they need a hand."

I went inside, prepared for culinary disaster, but a fruit flan, obviously purchased from Jenny's Bakery in town, was sitting abandoned on the kitchen counter ...

... while Jack pressed Priya up against the fridge and kissed her.

When the back door closed behind me, they sprang apart, both looking at the floor, the walls—anywhere but at me. Priya smoothed down her skirt while Jack tucked his shirt back into his pants.

"Umm ..." I said. "Sorry to interrupt. I thought there might be a problem, but it looks like everything's sweet."

Priya gave Jack a shy smile, and they both laughed. The tension dissolved as Jack ran a hand over his short hair. "Ah, yeah. You could say that. Dessert is coming right up."

"Want me to take it out and, ah, leave you to it?"

Jack's colour deepened. "We'll, um, be there in a minute."

"We're practising," Priya told me.

I raised an eyebrow as I scooped up the flan and the small plates next to it. "It looked like you pretty much had the hang of it."

She laughed. "I was concerned that we might have trouble persuading my mother that we were for real this time. So Jack said we should practise being persuasive."

I nodded at the back door. "Want to get that for me?"

Jack sprang to open it. His whole face was glowing, and he couldn't stop staring at Priya.

"Congratulations, guys," I said drily. "I think you've nailed it."

Priya caught his hand and dragged him outside with me. I was close enough to hear when she leaned in and whispered to him, "We can practise some more later."

Jack blushed adorably. I had a feeling I was going to see a lot of Jack's blushes in the weeks to come, and I smiled. My friends were happy. *I* was happy. Life in Sunny Bay was never dull, but Curtis was right.

Moving here was the best thing I'd ever done.

THE END

IF YOU WOULD LIKE to read an exclusive free story about Charlie and the gang and the Great Pavlova Disaster, plus hear about new releases, special deals and other book news, sign up for my newsletter at www.emeraldfinn.com.

Reviews and word of mouth are vital for any author's success. If you enjoyed *Family, Friends and Fatalities*, please take a moment to leave a short review where you bought it. Just a few words sharing your thoughts on the book would be extremely helpful in spreading the word to other readers (and this author would be immensely grateful!).

THE LIFE'S A BEACH SERIES

Welcome to beautiful Sunrise Bay, where the beach is hot and the corpses are cold

Sun, Sand and Slaughter: Charlie moves to idyllic Sunrise Bay for a fresh start, but discovers trouble in paradise when her aunt's friend dies in suspicious circumstances.

Veil, Vows and Vengeance: Charlie's photographing a beach wedding. Beautiful bride: check. Gorgeous weather: check. Dead guest: definitely not part of the plan.

Blondes, Bikinis and Betrayal: Charlie faces a puzzling case of double trouble. A woman is murdered and her twin sister is distraught ... or is she?

Santa, Surf and Sapphires: Someone in Sunrise Bay is on Santa's naughty list when a sapphire necklace disappears in the middle of a charity auction.

Family, Friends and Fatalities: When a woman falls to her death from a hotel balcony, Charlie is drawn into the case by a missing shoe.

Acknowledgements

Thanks to my husband Mal and daughter Jen for beta reading. Also to Mal for giving me the idea for the murder.

And a big thank-you to Isabella Pickering for stepping in as editor and making me look good!

ABOUT THE AUTHOR

Emerald Finn loves books, tea, and chocolate, not necessarily in that order. Oh, and dogs. And solving mysteries with the aid of her trusty golden retriever. No, wait. That last bit might be made up.

In fact, Emerald herself is made up, though it's absolutely true that she loves books, tea, chocolate, and dogs. Emerald Finn is the pen name of Marina Finlayson, who writes books full of magic and adventure under her real name. She shares her Sydney home with her kids, a large collection of dragon statues, and the world's most understanding husband.

Printed in Great Britain
by Amazon